GUNPLAY OVER LAREDO

Laredo was a boom town with more than its share of villains. Chief wild man was Luke Starn, hell-bent on making a dishonest fortune in the shortest time. But Chet Wayne, the quick shooting deputy sheriff was equally determined to keep law and order. Conflict was inevitable, and soon there was gunplay over Laredo.

Books by Norman Lazenby
in the Linford Western Library:

SINGING LEAD
A FIGHTIN' HOMBRE

NORMAN LAZENBY

GUNPLAY OVER LAREDO

Complete and Unabridged

LINFORD
Leicester

First published in Great Britain in 1952 by
J. Coker
London

First Linford Edition
published September 1991

British Library CIP Data

Lazenby, Norman A. (Norman Austin)
    Gunplay over Laredo.—Large print ed.—
Linford western library
    I. Title
    823.914

    ISBN 0–7089–7091–5

Published by
F. A. Thorpe (Publishing) Ltd.
Anstey, Leicestershire
Set by Words & Graphics Ltd.
Anstey, Leicestershire
Printed and bound in Great Britain by
T. J. Press (Padstow) Ltd., Padstow, Cornwall

1

HE came up out of the desert on a horse as tired as he was. From his saddle-horn a rope led to another plodding horse. Dust and sweat caked the man's face. He slouched in the saddle, tired and bitter. The sun slanted redly, raising shimmering heat-waves. Nothing stirred in the desert west of Laredo. Not even a rattler moved out of the path of the two plodding horses.

Chet Wayne slowly put out a hand to the water canteen strapped to the saddle. He undid the buckle and then halted his horse. He slid down stiffly from the saddle and moved around to the horse's mouth. He pulled out the cork from the canteen and allowed water to trickle on to the palm of his hand.

Almost before the water collected, the

cayuse had licked it up with a raspy tongue.

"Thet's yore ration, Blackie," muttered Chet Wayne. "Now fer the other hoss. Ain't right yuh should git all the water, amigo!"

He strode around and approached the other animal. He emptied the water on to his hand again-down to the last slow drop. The horse snuffled over the hand, wiping every drop up.

Chet Wayne rammed the cork back.

"All right, hosses," he grunted. "Let's git goin' fer Laredo again. Ain't more'n five miles now, I reckon."

It was typical of the man that he had carefully rationed the water to the last moment, carefully considering the horses before his own wants. Chet Wayne was a big man, hard muscled and heavy boned. He was not unusual in a country where men were bred tough. He was just a hombre on a trail.

And there were men in roaring Laredo whom he wanted to meet.

Words would be few and probably lead to gunplay.

Laredo was a boom town. The railroad gangs were just thirty miles away, skirting the Texas-Mexico border, and the Irish labourers rode into town by means of a bogey-truck most every night. Ranchers, cattle-buyers and cowpokes made the town their rendezvous, and it was inevitable that the hangers-on should be there, too. Gamblers, wasters, robbers and honkytonk girls made Laredo streets infamous.

Sure there were decent men and women. The boom town had a church and stores. There was a preacher to carry out weddings and burials, and a doctor to see that some of the victims of shooting affrays lived. There was a sheriff — one Tom Hudson by name. He had been Sheriff of Laredo long before the railroad gangs pushed the steel tracks over the plains and through the mountains that sided Laredo. Tom Hudson had kept the office longer than any other Laredo sheriff. But there were

3

some who were bitterly dissatisfied with Tom Hudson of late.

Chet Wayne, as deputy sheriff, was one of the men who were dissatisfied. For the past seven months, ever since he had taken over the office from his predecessor who had died because of Colt slugs, he had been grim, wary and suspicious. Tom Hudson's actions had induced those inward feelings.

But there was nothing as yet which Chet could pin down. So far it was just sheer dissatisfaction with Tom Hudson's conduct as a sheriff. It was incredible, but Tom had allowed chances of rounding up desperadoes to pass. He had avoided gunplay in certain parts of the town. He had ignored complaints of rustling and gold stealing. The change had come over Tom Hudson gradually. No man had been able to indicate the time of the change of character; and so far it had not been possible to hog-tie the sheriff on any specific charge.

There was just this uneasy dissatisfaction with the sheriff's ways of working.

The evening sun raised heat shimmers over Laredo as Chet Wayne rode slowly into the town. There was a smell of sweating horse and hot saddle-leather about him. He figured he badly needed a wash and a shave. He was not a rannigan who liked desert dust and three-day beards. Most time he was a hombre who was right particular about his appearance.

Chet figured to ride straight to the sheriff's office, put the horse in the livery and tell the Mex wrangler to look after them. After that Chet intended to spruce up, get the weariness out of his bones in his room on top of the sheriff's office. Then he figured to talk to Tom Hudson.

But this plan was upset.

He had hardly reached the tie-rail outside the office building when a young rannigan strode grimly from a saloon porch. The buckeroo went bullheaded across the dusty street. His hands hovered over the tops of fancy Colts. There was anger in every line of his iron-hard body.

He paced up to Chet Wayne and grabbed at the deputy's arm. He tugged. Chet could not shake off the grip, and so he was forced to dismount. He faced the angry rannigan.

"If you want to talk, Rory Blain, yuh don't have to pull me off my hoss!"

"That's Bernard's cayuse!" flared the other. Fury brought his weather-tanned face to an angry red. "Yuh killed Bernard! Yuh brought his hoss back! Damn yuh fer a low gunslinger!"

"Bernard had it comin'," said Chet evenly and tiredly. "When a hombre holds up a bank an' rides out with stolen gold he's a wanted man, an outlaw. Yore brother did all that, an' then tried to drygulch me when I rode along his trail."

"Yuh durned liar! More likely yuh shot him in the back! Yuh couldn't ha' tracked Bernard in a lifetime!"

6

Chet Wayne's temper was shredded.

"Yuh're a hot-head, Rory Blain! Yuh'll end up like yore brother! I'm a-warning yuh! Yuh're playing around with a bunch of lawless rannigans an' you'll end up with Colt slugs or maybe a rawhide noose. You'll bring grief to yore sister."

"Yuh kin leave Jane's name out o' this!" snarled Rory Blain. "An' when she gits to hearin how yuh shot Bernard, she'll ride into town an' tell you jest what sort of skunk she figgers you are!"

Chet Wayne braced his shoulders. The buckeroo's hot, venomous words made him sick. Chet had not been afraid of Bernard Blain; he had ridden after the robber because it was his job. And Chet feared little that Rory Blain might throw up. But Jane Blain was a different proposition.

All during the thirty-six hours of riding back to Laredo his mind had been tormented by the nature of the words he should use in telling Jane that he had killed Bernard Blain. That had added to the ride across the baked desert.

Chet had visited Jane a number of times down at the Blain ranch, the Double X. Chet had liked to talk to the bright-eyed, brown-haired girl. Only once or twice had he tried to hint that her two hot-head brothers were heading for a trail of grief. And then Jane had flared with an outburst of family pride. She had defended Rory and Bernard with a lot of illogical, feminine excuses. Chet could not blame her. After that he had talked of other things when he had visited the ranch. They had found a lot in common in discussing the invasion of cholla cactus on to the impoverished spread and the way the few head of cattle broke down the banks of the water holes. Chet Wayne had a warm admiration for the girl in her fight against poor land. He had thought Jane liked him a lot. Slowly, because he was not a town dandy, he had figured on getting around to some mighty important questions concerning them both.

But now . . .

"I'll ride down an' explain everythin' myself to Jane," said Chet steadily.

"Yuh kin keep yore nose out o' our ranch!" came the rush of hate-filled words.

"I aim to tell her the truth," said Chet grimly. "She can judge after that. But I'd like Jane to hear my side of the story."

Rory Blain teetered on the balls of his feet. Swiftly his hands plucked at the buckle of his belt. In a second he swung the belted holster to the ground. Instantly he crouched and weaved vicious fists at Chet Wayne.

"Maybe yuh kin stand up to a dead man's brother!" snarled Rory. "I aim to smash yuh to pulp, Mister Lawman. Git offen them belts! I don't want a bullet in my back!"

Chet slowly unbuckled his belt. He thought the young rannigan was stupidly hot-headed. He was bent upon making a scene which wouldn't help anybody or prove anything. Had the setting not been a Laredo street, with witnesses already crowding the boardwalks and saloon porches, Rory Blain might have been tempted to use his guns, probably without any warning.

"Yuh're a fool," said Chet coldly. "A doggone pesky fool! Any damn feller in this town knows I just been doin' my duty when I rode out after yore brother."

"Maybe yuh ain't so handy with yore fists as yuh are with yore mouth an' hoglegs!" jeered Rory Blain.

He had noted Chet Wayne's exhausted condition. He knew he had only to goad the other man into a fight and then take advantage of the other's weariness to smash him up unmercifully.

"Maybe I can teach yuh some sense!" gritted Chet Wayne.

Even as his belt swung to the ground and he stepped clear, he knew he was attempting a grim task. He was bone-tired. It was the sort of weariness that only lack of sleep, terrible heat and many miles of glaring sand can induce. He was half-way to being licked before he started. Rory Blain, on the other hand, was a tough young rannigan with a night's sleep and good meals behind him. True, he had been drinking in the saloon as Chet had ridden into town, but that had merely added viciousness to this new spasm of hatred.

The hot-headed young buckeroo rushed in the moment Chet stepped to one side. So eager was he to inflict punishment that he ran into Chet's swiftly-raised fists.

Chet Wayne swung a right and left, hoping to sting his opponent and slow down the attack. Throwing out his bunched fists was like lifting lead weights. The blows landed, even as a ruthless fist slashed into his own face with fiery torment. Chet staggered even under the first blow. Desperately he dug his boots into the dust, slithering for a steady foundation. He swung his fists again, trying to pound at the jeering face just ahead.

A group of onlookers edged closer. A fight in Laredo's streets was nothing new, but free entertainment was never passed up. Some of the onlookers thought it was good to see a nosy lawman take a beating. Almost as many were grimly displeased, but there was nothing to be gained by intervention.

Chet Wayne felt pounding blows to the body force him back. He strove to get a fist rammed into Rory Blain's mocking face. He did connect with a right; heard the man grunt and knew with grim dismay that he had not hurt the hot-blooded buckeroo. Then a rain of retaliatory blows dazed all thought. Chet staggered back, fighting desperately with arms that felt like stones.

He knew that at any other time he could have punished Rory Blain and made the hombre sorry he had asked for a fight. But not this time. Those thirty-six hours after Bernard Blain had died in a fair gun-fight were telling on him: He was not the same man.

Chet was pounded right back to the rail outside the office. There he stopped, propped by the tie-rail. He kept up a guard with arms that weighed like lead and moved with the slowness of exhaustion.

Rory Blain closed in to beat Chet to submission. His young, rough face was contorted in triumph.

Fists whirled and hooked to Chet's jaw and body. Fists rammed through Chet's weary guard.

The deputy sheriff began to slide down. Only the tie-rail propped him up. Chet's riding boots dug and slithered in the dust while he fought back a dazed feeling. He did not know what his fists were doing. He had a strange feeling they did not belong to him. His arms were lumps of lead that were numb and useless.

Merciless blows slammed into him, jerking his head back in agony. Dust and sweat mingled with blood. And all the time Chet Wayne slid down and down.

Finally, he panted and lay prone. He made an effort to rise. He clawed for support from the tie-rail posts but he seemed to have no control over his hands. He slumped again in reaction.

Rory Blain grinned wickedly and stepped closer. An idea had entered his head.

As Chet sprawled, one hand was flung outwards. It was his right hand. The hand lay in the dust.

"Yuh won't take on any more gun-play, feller!" rasped Rory Blain.

He stepped close and raised his booted foot. The intention was clear. He aimed to stamp down hard on Chet's outstretched hand and so break the fingers. It was an old rough-house trick — a dirty frontier trick that only a rowdy like Rory Blain would adopt.

But even as the hot-head lifted his foot, a man stepped out of the crowd. He bumped into Rory Blain and knocked him at least two feet. Rory undoubtedly set both feet on ground — but it was mostly to balance himself!

"Thet ain't in the play, Blain!" snapped the other man.

The young buckeroo glared back.

"Cain't yuh stick to yore own bizness, Walt Carr?"

"Fair play is my bizness!" snapped the other, and he walked over to Chet and helped him up.

Chet Wayne gulped great lungfuls of air and felt the world steady again. He even started forward, but there was a resisting pressure on his arm. Walt Carr, a rancher from one of Laredo's outlying spreads, was warning him that enough was enough. Chet lay back against the tie-rail.

"Git goin', Blain," rapped Walt Carr. "Unless yuh want to see the hoose-gow from the inside for assaultin' a deputy sheriff!"

Rory Blain bent down to buckle on his gun belt. He kicked Chet's belt over in his direction contemptuously. Chet walked forward stiffly. He bent slowly, picked up his gun belt and began to buckle it on. He stared sombrely at Rory Blain.

"Yuh an' me ain't finished, hombre," he said. "Yuh beat me — all right! Maybe the next time you won't be so blamed lucky!"

The crowd dispersed with plenty of sharp remarks and a few guffaws. Rory Blain swaggered back to the saloon, there to listen to some cheap praise at the bar.

Walt Carr stared at Chet.

"What you need is plenty of rest an' then somethin' good to eat. Say, is that true — yuh had to shoot Bernard Blain? That his hoss?"

"Yeah." Chet turned to the two patiently standing animals. "I brought back the hoss to prove Bernard Blain was dead. I had to shoot it out. What else kin yuh do when a man lays for yuh with a Winchester? I was mighty lucky to git him!"

"Good riddance." Walt Carr pushed back his Stetson. "Thet other hellion,

Rory, is slug-bait unless I miss my guess."

"Where's Tom Hudson?" asked Chet. He stared at the windows of the sheriff's office.

"Don't seem around. You go in an' git that shuteye. Lock the door an' sleep with a hogleg under yore pillow. Maybe yuh ain't so popular with some gents around here."

Chet wiped blood and sweat from his cheeks.

"As a matter o' fact, I reckon to see Jane Blain afore I think o' restin'. I want to talk to her afore the wrong story gits around."

And Chet led the two horses around to the livery at the rear of the sheriff's office.

Walt Carr shook his head doubtfully.

"There's a hombre who don't know when he's had enough!"

After seeing that Blackie, the big mare, and the other cayuse were going to get attention from the Mexican wrangler, Chet went to his room at

17

the top of the office building.

He stripped to the waist. He ran cold water from a jug into a wash-basin. He began to get rid of the mixture of blood, dust and sweat.

Some time later he shaved, wielding the long-handled razor with tired care. He really wanted to rest, but more than this need he wanted to see Jane. He just wanted to explain to her how fate had handed him an unpleasant duty. If he waited until the story reached her ears, the facts would be distorted. At the moment, all the town knew was the bare fact that the law had caught up with Bernard Blain, bank robber.

Fifteen minutes later Chet Wayne was a presentable hombre in clean trousers of brown material. A blue gaberdine shirt stretched across chest muscles. He had donned a new fawn Stetson. He had polished his boots until they shone with gleaming black again. He had wiped flecks of horse blood from his spurs. He wanted to get rid of the desert-tramp feeling entirely and so he donned leather, brass-studded cuffs for his wrists and then pulled on tight-fitting brown riding gloves. His last act was to fasten leather riding chaps around his brown trousers.

When he walked stiffly to the livery again, he was an example of the prosperous male of the frontier towns of the nineties.

The Mexican had a fresh horse waiting for him, as instructed previously. Chet swung into the clean saddle, noted the rifle boot was empty. He did not think it mattered right now. He had his Colts, and as always they were clean and oiled.

He rode along the dusty main stem, passing the false-fronted saloons and hotels. He skirted a stationary freight-wagon, and thought the railroad would make some difference to this trade. At the moment the saloons were not too full. Later the railroad workers would ride in on the bogey with their wild Irish songs. He could hear fiddlers hammering out music from a dance-hall nearby. Inside the gilded and red-plush place there would be a fair crowd. The percentage girls would be taking money or gold dust from the miners and cowpokes.

Chet stopped at a Chinese restaurant; tied his horse. He had to eat, and this was quicker than making something up in his room.

Some time later, after jerky beef and gravy, apple-tart and coffee, he went out and climbed to the saddle. He still felt pretty weary. He sat in the saddle for a moment and rolled a brown-paper cigarette. He lit the cigarette with a match and threw the match carefully into the dust. Then he jogged the horse onwards.

The Double X lay west of Laredo, about five miles out of town, along the vast valley. The ranch was mostly a strip of land parallel with the foothills and the grass was not so thick as those ranches that occupied the best parts of the great valley. At this time of the year the heat withered the land and only the cholla cactus and ocotillo flourished along with the purple sage.

Chet wondered what task had taken Tom Hudson out of town. Certainly the sheriff had been away from Laredo.

Wal, undoubtedly Sheriff Tom Hudson would hear about Bernard Blain and the rumpus with Rory.

Chet figured to watch Tom Hudson's reactions. He had a hunch that the sheriff would listen to the whole story with a grouse.

As a lawman, Tom Hudson should be pleased that a desperado had been rounded up; but he would not be. Chet Wayne could almost gamble on that hunch. Anyway, he would see. First there was this talk with Jane.

Chet allowed the fresh horse to canter briskly along the trail. He sat tall in the saddle in spite of the rotten tired feeling. The cuts on his face had closed. He had applied plenty of cold water. But there was a bruise on one cheek that would take time to heal.

Presently he had to leave the trail

and head across the browned land. The aroma of sage soon arose from under the horse's hoofs. He let the animal proceed at a full lope.

Soon the ranch buildings came into his sight. They nestled against a rise of land and were sheltered against the southern arc of the sun by a clump of cottonwoods. A defined trail ran to the ranch now. Along the way were one or two clumps of Joshua trees, those gaunt desert growths, and Chet instinctively slowed his horse as he approached a clump. He could see the Double X buildings nicely now. There was the yard rail, the corral and barn. The ranch-house was small and made of sawn logs. A porch ran around it and Chet could see the steps.

But he could see more than this. And he had instinctively slowed the horse because of this.

A man lounged against a post on the porch of the ranch-house. Even from this distance, Chet knew him. He recognized his lounging attitude and general build. He could not see the man's face, but he knew the galoot was Luke Starn.

Chet jigged the horse forward, slowly. He kept his eyes fixed on the distant porch. It was like a stage set in the glaring rays of the slanting sun.

Luke Starn was a man Chet disliked and suspected. He disliked him because the hombre was too shrewd and smooth and glib. And he suspected him because the man had no business or trade other than gambling and yet appeared to live well — in the tradition of the hard frontier man with easy money. Luke Starn drank plenty and paid for plenty of rotgut that never went down his own throat. He did not work. He liked to dress in store suits, imported from Chicago and east. He threw money away on the honky-tonk girls. Unlike the traditional gambler in the western cattle-towns, he carried twin Colts and not a small derringer in a vest pocket! Chet had heard the man owned property in Laredo. There was no crime in that, but for a man who did not work it seemed strange.

Chet kept on jigging the horse nearer to the ranch-house and then he suddenly saw another figure join Luke Starn on the porch.

He knew it was Jane Blain, and she was wearing her plaid shirt and blue levis tucked into riding boots. She often looked more like a boy than a girl. But Chet would know that figure from even a greater distance.

The next moment he was wishing he had ridden along later! For with a swift movement, Luke Starn had brought the girl close to him and was holding her in a close embrace.

Chet Wayne nearly halted the horse, but he let it walk slowly onward. Grim blue eyes stared at the ranch-house. He felt a queer, inward bitter pang. Was Jane allowing a wastrel like Luke Starn to hold her?

2

BEFORE Chet could really make up his mind about his course of action, the horse had approached nearer to the ranch and the two on the porch had seen him. They wheeled and stared, leaning on the porch rail as Chet rode up.

Chet Wayne figured his poker face was functioning. Not for his life did he want Jane to realize he had seen her in Luke Starn's embrace.

He realized there had been little in the action. And he had not been near enough to notice with what willingness Jane had allowed Luke Starn to hold her like that.

Still, the whole thing rankled. But there was nothing he could object to. Jane was a woman with personal freedom. She could pick her own friends — and, no doubt, her lover, too.

He did curse Luke Starn's presence. The last thing he wanted was to explain about Bernard in front of Luke Starn. The gambler's attitude towards all lawmen was one of amused contempt.

But he had to ride up.

Chet did not dismount after he had ridden through the open gate in the ranch-yard fence. He sat heavily in the saddle and nodded to Luke Starn. He could see the man's horse over by the corral. The animal was still blowing, so the man had not been long at the ranch!

"Howdy, Deputy! You lookin' fer bad men?" Starn seemed amused, as usual.

Chet seized the chance.

"I figured to talk to Miss Jane, kinda private," he hinted.

"Yeah? Well, amigo, you can see that I'm talkin' to her." There was a counter-hint.

Jane Blain spoke up.

"What do you want, Chet? Anythin' about Bernard?"

There was anxiety in her voice. She

knew that the deputy had ridden out after her brother. Rory had brought back the news, with boasts that Chet Wayne would never catch up with Bernard. He had not told Jane that Bernard had robbed a bank; he had vaguely mentioned Bernard was in trouble. Jane had heard later about Bernard's exploit and she had felt bitter about her wild brother's actions. She had waited in tense anxiety for news — and now here was Chet Wayne himself.

"Bernard got away, didn't he?" she said anxiously. "Sure, you couldn't trail him. He had too much start. Rory says you would never ride up on him."

She was trying to assure herself as much as anything.

Chet was silent for almost a minute. It was not part of his task to tell her how he had done without sleep and risked laming his splendid horse in the effort to diminish Bernard Blain's lead. And a man with a lame horse was as good as buzzard bait out in the baking desert. He had crossed the bad lands and caught up with Bernard Blain by exercise of sheer guts.

But that was not what he figured to tell the girl.

Jane stared at him fearfully.

"He did get away? Why don't you speak? He did get away, didn't he?"

Chet looked grimly at Luke Starn. The man's dark face had lost its amused expression. Chet thought he detected a look of anger. But it was only a momentary shade on the man's dark face and dark gleaming eyes. "I'll talk to yuh after yore visitor has gone, Jane," said Chet grimly.

Her woman's intuition leaped to conclusions — and they were the right ones!

"Bernard is dead! You killed him! I can see it on your face! Oh — oh — Gawd — "

Luke Starn had realized the truth, too, and that was why his face had changed expression.

"So yuh gunned the man down!" he grated.

Chet tried to stop the rot.

"Jane — I'd like to talk to yuh alone. Just give me a few minutes, Jane."

Her voice charged back at him, filled with anger.

"It's true! Answer me! You killed Bernard! Why don't you answer — you — gunslinger!"

"Look, Jane, I rode out here to talk to yuh, not fight. Say yuh'll lissen to me, Jane."

"Why don't you tell me the truth!" she almost screamed. "Berny's dead! You've killed him! Why don't you say that?"

Chet said huskily: "All right. That's the truth. Yore brother is dead. He laid for me with a rifle an' I had to crawl up to him with Colts. It was a fair fight, Jane. He was a wanted man. He was resisting arrest, an' more'n that he was figurin' to leave me for dead. It was him or me!"

The girl gave a choking gasp, and then darted back to the ranch-house door. In another second, swift as a wild-cat, she appeared on the porch again.

She held a gun in her hand, and she pointed it straight at Chet Wayne.

"Git off this ranch! Before I kill you!"

The gun did bark. A slug raised a little dust cloud near Chet's horse. Jane had triggered under the impulse of her terrible anger.

Chet controlled the animal as it crowhopped in fright. He was deadly calm now.

"I'm a-goin', Jane. Just wanted to tell you the story myself. Too bad this hombre had to be here an' tangle my loop. Just a tip, Jane. Maybe yuh can straighten up Rory. If yuh can't, he'll head for the same end as Bernard."

He wheeled his horse and cantered out of the yard. His broad back was a target and he knew it. But he also knew the folk in the territory might be rough, but they did not shoot a man in the back. Only a few no-good characters would lower their own self-esteem to that. Jane would never shoot him, no matter how hot-tempered she was. And Luke Starn had a lot to lose in killing a deputy sheriff. Tom Hudson might be weak these days, but beyond Laredo there was a Town Marshal in Abilene and Judge Tarrant in whose circuit the two towns lay.

He sent the horse over the semi-arid land at a full lope. He hunched down in the saddle, bone tired now and dispirited. His plans had misfired. Jane would hate him now. The friendship that had developed between them, despite all difficulties the Blain brothers had put in its way, had encountered a terrible obstacle. For his part, he wanted to help Jane, wanted to have a courtship. But she regarded him now as the man who had killed her brother. It was a tough break.

He had not liked the little he had seen concerning Jane and Luke Starn. Ordinarily, he would not have left the girl with the man. But she had sent him packing at the end of a Colt!

What damn fools women were to even talk to hombres like Starn! And he could not even stop her!

Chet thought the time had arrived for that sleep he so badly needed. A man could go so long. He thought that maybe four hours would set him up. And somewhere along the line he wanted to talk to Tom Hudson. After all, the man was sheriff!

Some time later he cantered the horse into Laredo and made straight for the sheriff's office.

He led the horse into the livery, and then walked into the office on the ground floor. The sheriff's office was one of the few buildings in the town that was made of bricks. On the ground floor lay the office proper, with four barred cells at one end. 'Wanted' posters were tacked to walls. A glass case held a number of old guns. To one side of the office and jail lay two rooms which served Tom Hudson as living quarters, seeing that he was a bachelor.

When Chet walked in, he saw the sheriff sitting at his desk, scanning three new 'wanted' posters which had been sent him from the County Court office.

"Take a look at these galoots," grunted Tom Hudson. "This town is getting thick with these border rannigans."

Chet sat down on a seat and looked at the posters. He did not know the three men described.

"I heard about Bernard Blain," muttered Tom Hudson without looking at Chet. "Wal, every jigger has to get his, I reckon."

"Did yuh hear about the fight I had with Rory?" asked Chet.

"Yeah. It got around. Keep away from thet ornery young cuss, Chet. It don't do no good stirrin' up trouble."

"Sure. But that young gink tackled me. I had to fight, Tom, an', hell, I'm about all in!"

"Git yoreself some shuteye," muttered the sheriff.

Tom Hudson was a grizzled man of about forty eight years and he was of medium height, broad build. His hair was a greyish stubble. Right now his grey eyes never met Chet's blue ones.

"Did yuh find the money Bernard Blain lifted from thet bank?" asked Tom Hudson.

"He must ha' cached it somewhere. Wasn't near him — after the shootin'. Reckon thet money will never be found now."

"Did you search the galoot afore yuh buried him?"

"Sure. Nothin' much on him 'cept the 'makings' and his matches. No letters. Anyway, I reckon those wild Blain hombres ain't much hand at readin'. I left his guns to mark the spot. I brought his hoss back to prove the feller is dead."

"No letters." Tom Hudson seemed a little easier in mind. His slate grey eyes even flicked to Chet.

"Not a durned thing," said Chet. "He even rode out so fast, he hadn't a grubstake. He must ha' figured to shoot jack rabbits — an' that's kinda crazy."

"Mebbe he didn't figure to ride out."

"That could be," agreed Chet. "Wal, doggone it, I'm so tired I could sleep on one of them Army Cavalry camels! I'm a-goin' up to my roof. Call me if yuh want me, Sheriff." But it was dark when Chet awoke. And he wakened swiftly and alarmingly. There was only a second of warning. His sense of danger leaped like a jag of lightning in that second.

He awakened and rolled off the bed all in the one movement. So quick was the action that he thudded to the bare boards.

Chet Wayne sprang up and saw the dark shape over his bed. The intruder had still not reacted. The man had not straightened yet.

Chet saw something glint in the pale light that came through the window.

He recognized it as a knife. Then he leaped right across the bed at the stranger!

It was an angry, impulsive leap. And this time Chet Wayne was not a tired man.

His guns were slung on a chair and not so quickly reached as the intruder himself. Chet Wayne just acted without even thinking. There was not time for thought.

He had his hands grappling with the man in no time at all. With the initial thrust, he shoved the man across the room. Then one grim fist snaked to the wrist holding the knife.

The man had reacted from a stealthy intruder to a man who had to fight for his life. Light glinted again on the blade as the man strove to use it. But Chet gripped the wrist. He forced the arm up and then backwards. With his other hand he reached for the galoot's windpipe.

They fought for some seconds in this manner, and then the intruder could hold the knife no longer. The blade fell to the boards and got kicked to one side. Chet slid his hand from the man's wrist and attempted to get a firmer grip with two hands around the galoot's neck.

The intruder was having the worst of the encounter. He had lost his opportunity. Now he was fighting for his life. Chet was squeezing the wind out of his neck. The man clawed at Chet's hands with strong finger-nails that gouged the flesh. But Chet did not relent.

He could not determine the identity of the man. It was not Rory Blain. He did not know why he should be attacked. That is, he did not know the exact reason. Naturally, a deputy sheriff had enemies. This jigger evidently had some real bad feeling for him to creep into the room at night with a knife!

The man was gasping when all of a sudden Chet decided to throw him to the floor. Chet did not want such a death on his hand. If death had to be ad ministered, he liked it dished up with Colts in a fair fight. He did not want to kill a man with his hands.

So he flung the man down. The rannigan was almost choked to death in any case.

Chet hurled him from him. He heard the thud as the man hit the floor and a strange, sharp cry. Chet stood over the man for a moment, still angry and slightly breathless. The man rolled once and then did not move.

Chet waited and then thought there was something queer about the man's motionless attitude. He bent over him. He rolled the man.

And then he saw what had happened. The dropped knife had somehow been kicked and fallen into a deep crack between two floor-boards. But the blade had protruded. It was a strange thing to happen.

The man had fallen on to the blade and had been impaled. As Chet moved the man, blood welled out of the wound between the shoulder-blades.

Chet moved across the room and found matches. He lit the lamp, and then turned to the dead man.

He found himself looking at a typical border breed. He had never seen the hombre before. But Laredo was full of this type. He was a swarthy breed, with black hair and sideboards. He had a steeple shaped hat, but wore a cowpoke's flapping vest and dirty shirt.

"Now who the heck sent yuh to kill me?" muttered Chet Wayne.

Some hunch told him the man was a hireling. To the best of his knowledge, he had never crossed this man before, so the desire to kill could not be part of a personal feud. The more he thought about it, the more it seemed likely that the breed had been hired to kill. Being a breed, he had chosen the knife. There was only one thing wrong with the scheme — and that was the breed had encountered death instead of the victim selected! But from Chet's point of view, the event had turned out fair enough!

"Yuh're a customer for Doc Harper an' boothill!" muttered Chet again.

Doc Harper, Laredo's medico, had to examine any corpse found in the town and write out a sort of certificate. He was often a busy man. Often when Doc Harper was finished, the gravedigger on boothill was the next to be interested in the customer!

Chet looked at the window on the other side of the room. It was open because the nights were warm even though the earth cooled quickly during the nocturnal hours. But Chet had not left it so much open as all that. The border ruffian had evidently scaled the wall outside and entered by the window.

Ordinarily, Chet thought he would have heard the first sound; but he had been in deep sleep.

Well, the slumber was over for the time being!

There was work to do. Chet hauled the dead man down the stairs and out by a back door to the yard at the rear of the building. There he unceremoniously dumped the body. Then he went in search of Doc Harper. Even in a lawless town like Laredo, bodies had to be disposed of. After the Doc had finished, it would be the gravedigger's task. And good riddance.

Sheriff Tom Hudson was not in the office when Chet looked in. That was not surprising. Tom Hudson spent some time in the Gold Nugget, a saloon half-way down the dusty main stem.

Doc Harper might be in the saloon, too. Many of the town's leading men gathered there. But first Chet figured to go over to the Doc's house.

He walked over. The glare of yellow light spilled from the many saloons. The stores were shut. An occasional horseman rode past, a belated cowboy riding in from the distant spreads, bent on a night's drinking and gambling. The music from the dance hall was stronger than ever. Maybe the fiddlers were drunk! Frequently the batwing doors of a saloon would swing out and a man would lurch through to a background of rowdy laughter from the bar. Chet thought nothing of the night. He had been reared to the life

41

of the west, first as a kid on a ranch where a kindly boss had seen that he went to school part-time. Then a few years roaming Texas to the borders of Arizona and Mexico. He had been top-hand, stage driver and bounty-hunter. Then he had settled in Laredo, worked as a cowboy and attended the town's council meetings. He had been a councilman and then, finally, deputy sheriff.

Chet Wayne came to Doc Harper's house, a white clapboard home with a picket fence and a garden that struggled against the road dust. He knocked on the door.

There was no immediate answer. Chet stepped to the side of the house to look at the windows. The shutters were not in place, and the moment he looked at the light it went out!

Chet stared at the blank pane for a moment; then he walked slowly to the door again. He knocked again.

He waited for an answer but there was no activity from inside the house.

With a puckered brow, Chet walked around the little home. Quietly he tried a side door, but it was locked. He thought it was darned queer. No one answered the door; yet there was someone inside!

Maybe Doc Harper was bent upon having a quiet night with his books! But why put out the light? The old galoot could be going to his bed, of course. But it was early as yet and early nights were not the Doc's usual habit.

Chet Wayne decided to retreat to the other side of the road and stand in the gloom between two store buildings.

He was wondering if the light would show again from the Doc's home. Was someone watching him and would the oil lamp be lit again the moment he disappeared?

If that happened, it could only mean that Doc Harper wanted to avoid company that night. He did not want callers. The old galoot was pretending to be away from home!

Chet stood in the darkness for some

minutes. Puzzled, he was just about to walk away back to the centre of the town when he discerned the door of the little house open.

Chet stood rigidly in the dark. There was some thing queer about the setup.

He thought he could make out three men moving in front of the house. They were in the dark and nothing was discernible.

Chet decided to walk forward. So far as he was concerned, he had official business with Doc Harper. He wanted to see him about the dead man destined for boothill. And if the persons ahead did not include Doc there was a tangle that ought to be investigated.

He crossed the road again with swift strides.

The group noticed him or they heard the jingle of his spurs.

A gun roared across the road suddenly. Chet heard the whine of the slug past his head. Orange flame slashed the darkness.

He knew he had done a damfool

thing in walking out minus his guns. But he had intended simply to ask the Doc to look at the dead man. He had not expected to be away more than minutes from the sheriff's office. Now he had run into this, and he was unprepared.

Chet flattened to the road. Another shot whizzed over him and sounded ominously in the night air.

Chet jerked his head up as he crouched in the road. He saw the two men hustling a smaller man between them. They ran for the deep blackness between two hay and corn stores.

A swift hunch told Chet that the small hombre was Doc Harper. And by the same token he knew the Doc was being hustled away to hitched horses.

The whole thing seemed like more lawlessness. He did not understand it. It looked as if Doc Harper was being kidnapped!

Chet spent not a second in useless conjecture. He had no guns, but he leaped up again after the first two shots and made for the men. As he ran he weaved erratically on the road, for he half expected more snap shots.

The weaving probably saved his life, for two shots exploded together — from two guns. The lead went wide of Chet. The flame leapt from the dark pool near the hay and corn stores.

The next instant a rapid tattoo of hoofs sounded in the air. Two horses stampeded out of the alley. One animal bore a double load. The horses rushed off at a full lope, raising a cloud of hoof dust.

Chet flung after them rather futilely. Then he stopped and cursed grimly.

If only he had strapped on his guns before leaving the office! But he had not. It was proof that a law-man had to live with his guns. There were some harmless cowpokes and ranchers, not to mention store-keepers, who never packed a Colt. But apparently that was not for a deputy sheriff!

Chet spun on his heel. He was sure that the small man who had been bustled off was Doc Harper. It was a kidnap. He couldn't guess at the reasons. But maybe the Doc's life was in danger.

He raced down the dusty stem. First he wanted his guns and then he had to rouse Tom Hudson — probably from the Gold Nugget. All this might take time. Maybe he should get his guns and his horse and ride out in the hope of locating the kidnappers!

The issue was settled for Chet Wayne when he raced into the office. Sheriff Tom Hudson was at the desk, staring at one of the new 'wanted' posters. He jerked his head as Chet rushed in.

"Yuh're in a blamed hurry?"

"Two galoots just kidnapped Doc Harper!" snapped Chet. "Git two hosses, Tom! I'm a-goin' for my hoglegs!"

And then he raced up the stairs.

He did not see Tom Hudson expel his breath in a terrible sigh; nor did he see the expression of dismay on the grizzled sheriff's face. Tom Hudson seemed to slump a little and hold the attitude for a few seconds. Then he turned and, moving with increased haste, went to the door that led around to the livery.

When Chet raced back to the stable, he found two horses with saddles ready for the final cinch. The Mex wrangler was not in the livery, having a date with a frowsy senorita in a cantina!

Seconds later they rode down the main stem, past Doc Harper's house. They did not stop to investigate the house.

Chet realized, even as it was, the chances of stumbling across the two kidnapping hombres was rather remote. It was really dark that night, and the moon had yet to soar into the sky.

Sheriff Tom Hudson and Chet rode down the trail which the kidnappers must have taken. Soon the outlying buildings of Laredo were left behind. It was dark and silent out here on the lonely trail. They could not see or sense any movement of horse or man. Maybe a moon would have made some difference, but the Old Man was not obliging that night!

Finally, they reined in the horses and halted on the trail. They listened intently and stared around at the dark landscape. They had the senses of trail-wise men, but there was nothing to give them a lead. Their horses were blowing slightly; a cooling breeze moved over the land and in the distance a coyote howled mournfully.

"Yuh cain't track men in the night!" growled Tom Hudson. "Now who the heck would want to kidnap Doc Harper? Are yuh shore he's bin kidnapped? Yuh ain't told me much."

"Guess there hasn't bin much time," retorted Chet. "But it's like this, Sheriff. A jigger climbed to my room while I was havin' thet bit of shut-eye, an' tried to slit me with a knife. I reckon this hombre was plumb unlucky because he got skewered himself. He's dead. Right now the body's in the yard, back o' the office. I went along to see the Doc, figgered to git him to look at this dead

49

gink. Then I ran into a queer play. I shore wish to hell I'd had my hoglegs with me!"

And Chet concluded by telling how he encountered the men hustling Doc Harper away into the night.

"Some o' the things that happen in this doggone town are plumb fixed to drive a man crazy!" complained Tom Hudson. "There just ain't no law an' order. Maybe I should ask Judge Tarrant to git some Texas Rangers sent hyar — or mebbe we could use some Army Cavalry."

"Yuh'd only git that help when there's riots!" said Chet sharply. "We can handle this." He paused and added grimly: "We ought to be able to handle it."

Tom Hudson sat low in the saddle and seemed to glower.

"Let's git back!" rapped Chet. "Maybe a posse would be the best thing. The folks ought to know Doc Harper's bin kidnapped. He's a valuable man. There ain't another doctor until yuh git to

Abilene — an' that jigger is better when he's workin' on hosses!"

"I guess yuh're right," muttered Tom Hudson.

"Thinkin' o' doctors," went on Chet grimly, "I got a hunch Doc Harper has been hustled away jest because he is a medical man."

"Yeah?"

"Shore. Makes sense, don't it?"

"Then maybe he ain't in real danger," returned Tom Hudson.

Chet fancied he detected relief in the sheriff's voice.

"Maybeso. But that don't give jiggers the right to hustle a citizen out o' his house."

They fed spur steel to the horses. They thundered back to town. The swift clop-clop of hoofs on dust brought them back to the main stem where light spilled from so many buildings.

Chet now held the opinion that Doc Harper had been hustled away to see some badly injured man who could not be moved. But the rustlers had forced the Doc to accompany them. To Chet's mind that meant the man who needed medical attention was a person outside the law.

He held to the above hunch because there had to be some valid reason for the Doc's kidnapping. Only the moon-crazy threatened a doctor.

Chet Wayne and Tom Hudson went into the Gold Nugget and spread the news around. There were many growls of disapproval. Two particular friends of Doc Harper went stamping out for horses and guns. Another man hurried off to visit another saloon where old patients of Doc Harper's might be interested. Doc Harper, despite his eccentricities, was well liked.

In a town like Laredo a doctor was an important possession. Even the utterly lawless would pause before killing a doctor — because there was no knowing when the medical man's services would be required!

Feeling dissatisfied, Chet walked out

on to the boardwalk just outside the Gold Nugget. He stopped to roll a cigarette from the makings. As he lighted the smoke, his mind was busy with his problems.

Two events had happened swiftly. A hired border breed had been sent to kill him. He felt someone was behind that unpleasant mission. Someone wanted him dead. Now who, in particular, could that be?

Then Doc Harper had been practically kidnapped. Whether the old hombre was in danger, no one could really determine. The fact was, forceful tactics like this could not be tolerated.

Chet stepped forward and then halted as an old man waddled from the hitching rail and stopped before him.

Even in the poor light outside the saloon, Chet could make out the dirty range clothes the man wore, the unkempt whiskers and the bright black eyes that regarded him keenly.

"Howdy!" greeted the waddy. "You the deputy, huh?"

The bright eyes fell to the badge on Chet's shirt.

"I'm the deputy," agreed Chet, and he made to step around the old fellow.

The waddy shifted his chewing tobacco so that he could speak more rapidly.

"Me, I'm Ezra Sloan. Jest an old hombre on the trail. Yuh lookin' fer some jiggers who jest rode out east? One o' 'em had a 'nother feller double-up on his hoss. I jest rode into this town. I jest heerd yuh were lookin' for these hellions."

"Did you see 'em?" demanded Chet, and he halted again.

"Yep. Shore did. Shore were feedin' rowels to them critters! An' one o' them fellers lost his hat. I picked it up. Yessir — never know when a new hat might be kinda useful, though I reckon to keep the one I got fer a lawng time!"

"Hat, huh?" Chet was slightly disappointed. "Yuh didn't see which trail they took?"

"Kinda dark, Mister," retorted Ezra Sloan. "Yuh want to look at this hat?"

"Yeah, I guess so."

The old-timer stepped back to the hitching rail and rummaged in a saddlebag. His horse was as dusty as himself and looked in need of fodder and water. Then Ezra Sloan stepped up to Chet again and thrust out a fine new Stetson.

Chet stared at it.

The hat had a distinctive band of rattlesnake skin. Chet remembered where he had last seen it.

Rory Blain had worn the hat earlier that evening. He had downed it with his gunbelt in order to fight!

Chet turned the hat, looked inside. As if willing to check, the name stared up at him, scrawled in ink.

"Rory Blain. Double X."

3

TWO horses galloped through the night and approached the shack set in the bluff. To one side of the shack was the remains of derelict mining gear — a rough wooden winch and some broken tubs. On the other side of the shack was the mouth of a tunnel into the bluff.

The two horses had galloped hard for nearly seven miles, and one animal bore a double load. As they came close to the cabin, the animals were reined in, snorting and blowing. The riders dismounted. One of them grabbed the arm of the smallish man who had been a passenger.

"All right, Doc, yuh ain't a-comin' to any harm if yuh jest behave yoreself!"

"Damn yuh both!" snapped Doc Harper. "When a man is hustled out of his own home to fix some no good son-of-a-snake, I figure that's the durned limit! Let me tell yuh, I'm accustomed to bein' asked to attend a patient!"

"Fer Gawd's sake, button yore lip!" snapped the other rider. It was Rory Blain, and he was in an unpleasant mood. For one thing he had recognized Chet Wayne down in the town, outside the Doc's house. He had slung lead at the deputy and was disgruntled because he had missed. So he had lost a chance to even up with his enemy.

"Let's git this hombre into the shack," said the first rannigan.

"Shore. Jest hitch up the hosses, Mulaney."

Rory Blain waited until the man named Mulaney had whipped reins over a post and then, together, they walked up to the broken-down porch that surrounded the shack.

A man was waiting in the shadows of the porch.

Rory Blain and Mulaney were not surprised to see him, and there were muttered greetings.

"Yuh got the Doc, all right?"

"Shore. No trouble. Except that pesky deputy had to stick his nose into it."

"Chet Wayne?"

"Yeah. Who else?" Rory was pretty sour.

The man on the porch muttered angrily.

"Holy hell, I paid Petrillo to — " The words ceased in an angry curse.

"Yuh got somethin' worryin' you, Starn?" inquired Rory Blain.

"Forget it," snapped Luke Starn. "It's just somethin' I remembered. All right, git the Doc in to see Dan."

The next few moments were spent in ushering Doc Harper into the badly lighted cabin. The door was shut after the party entered. A heavy cross-bar was put into place.

Doc Harper shrugged the two men free. They released his arms, and the little Doc began dusting his store suit and muttering threats under his white moustache.

Across the solitary cabin of the room,

a man lay on a rough bunk. He was covered with a dirty saddle blanket. His breathing was laboured and interposed with harsh groans.

"That why you've dragged me out hyar?" barked Doc Harper.

"Yeah. Look at him. Fix him up." Luke Starn snapped the directions at Doc Harper.

"What's wrong with him? Slug-trouble, I reckon?"

"Yuh're the Doc!" sneered Luke Starn. "As a matter o' fact, you're right. Dan's trouble is he's got more'n one slug in him. Any more damned chunks o' lead an' he'd be worth melting down! Haw, haw! I figger that's a hell of a joke! But git a looksee at Dan. His real name is Daniel Grig, an' he don't like sheriffs or docs!"

Doc Harper folded his arms.

"I usually get paid for my work, Mister Starn. But I haven't said I'll look at this hombre yet. What if I don't like the idee of fixin' up this cuss so that he can get into more gun-trouble?"

Dark eyes lost their derisive humour and snapped at the old medical man.

"Yuh'll do as yuh're told! Yuh don't want to git hurt. Jest work on Dan an' do it good."

"When I git back to town I'll report this to the sheriff!" rapped the Doc.

"So what! Report what the hell yuh like to the sheriff! What yuh gonna say? All yuh have to do is fix up a hurt man."

"Yuh're running mighty close to lawlessness, Mister Starn! You an' Rory Blain. What are yuh up to with this wounded man? How did this Dan Grig get hurt? And Mulaney hyar — I figure he's an owl hoot if ever I clapped eyes on one. A wanted man, I reckon. I figure to tell the sheriff plenty, Mister Starn."

Luke Starn walked around the room and thumbed his belt.

"Quit yappin' an' git to work. This galoot might die on yuh. It don't matter what yuh tell Sheriff Hudson. That old gink don't hear so good these days."

With this enigmatic remark, Luke

Starn impelled Doc Harper over to the man on the bunk. Dan Grig opened pain-filled eyes that stared briefly at the doctor. Then he began to curse him!

"So yuh got thet old horse-doctor! Hell, he couldn't take slugs outa a barn door! Gimme a shot o' rotgut! Blast thet stage guard! When I git around agen, I'll root him out an' fill his guts full o' lead. S'help me, he — "

Luke Starn clapped a hand over the man's mouth.

"Just quit beatin' yore gums, Grig! Remember, I got yuh a Doc. That shows yuh what I do for a man. Now quit yappin'! Yuh say too blamed much."

Doc Harper was shrewdly remembering every word. There was significance behind the few verbal crumbs, but naturally mere words were not evidence that amounted to much. They could be brushed aside, ignored or denied.

"D'yuh expect me to dig out .45 slugs with my fingers?" barked Doc Harper.

Rory Blain went over to the door and picked up a leather bag.

"I didn't forget. Yore black bag, Doc!"

Using a few swear-words he had almost forgotten, Doc Harper decided he would have to get on with the task.

But while he examined the wounded man, his thoughts were grimly busy. He got the idea that Daniel Grig had been shot by a stage guard. Heaven only knew what had happened to the stage-coach rifle carrier.

Doc Harper had not heard of any stage hold-up that day. The Concord had rolled into Laredo that evening on the trip from Abilene, and he had not heard of any attempted hold-up.

He did not understand. But undoubtedly Dan Grig was badly wounded.

Doc Harper supposed when the railroad took over all freight and passengers the hold-ups would be different. Why, some of these new locomotives could take a gradient at twenty-five miles an hour. That would sure give the bandits something to think about!

There was silence in the cabin while Doc Harper worked. Once the medic had started, he gave full attention to the task of getting the slugs out of the man's body. Warm water was brought to him. Doc Harper grimaced at the dirty piece of cloth that had to serve as a towel. He opined that if Dan Grig lived to kill other men and did not die of gangrene, he would be a pretty lucky devil.

Finally, Doc Harper's work was completed.

"He's got to rest an' be looked after for a few days," he said ironically.

Luke Starn came close, thumbs hooked near his twin Colts.

"And what are yore plans, Doc?" he asked smoothly.

"What do you think?" barked the other.

"I figger yuh might make a bit o' grief for us jiggers," said Luke Starn thoughtfully. "It wouldn't worry me what yuh told Tom Hudson. But there's others who ain't so agreeable.

63

A hombre name o' Chet Wayne, for instance. An' some o' those ranchers an' store-keepers figger the town ain't law abidin' enough. Yuh might git talkin' to them."

"What are yuh tryin' to threaten me with, Starn?" asked Doc Harper grimly.

"I ain't threatened yuh yet. But hyar it is. Keep yore lip buttoned, Doc. Yuh ain't seen nothin' hyar. Yuh don't know anythin' about this jigger Dan Grig."

"And if I don't?" asked the other quietly.

"Yuh'll be blasted afore yuh can git a mile. Yuh won't be able to stitch yoreself up, Doc. You'll be as dead as hell — if yuh talk. So play it smart, Doc. Just forget everythin'!"

Doc Harper breathed hard. He knew this was no idle warning. If he talked and made some grief for these men his life would not be worth a Mexican dollar.

"How do I git back to town?" he rapped.

"Yuh kin walk, Doc. Yuh ought to believe in exercise. So start walkin' right now. Seven-eight miles ain't so much I figger. Jest keeping on hoofin' an' yuh'll be back in town inside two hours or so. An' remember" — Luke Starn grabbed at the Doc's suit and dragged him close — "talk an' yuh're a dead man."

It was less than ten minutes later when Doc Harper set off from the derelict mine and the shack to walk back to distant Laredo.

In the cabin Dan Grig moaned and cursed.

"Yuh should ha' blasted thet little jigger! He'll bring a posse ridin' up hyar! They'll git me! Yuh know I'm wanted! Thet blamed deputy hates me like pisen! A posse would string me up!"

"Fer Gawd's sake shut up!" snarled Luke Starn. "The Doc won't talk. An' it's better to keep thet jigger alive. If he was found blasted, we'd have half the durned town out looking for sign.

Nope. The folks'ull settle down if the Doc's alive. Tom Hudson will let things slide. I got him fixed for that — you all know that."

"Yuh know best," agreed Mulaney, and he began to roll a cigarette unconcernedly.

Dan Grig fell to muttering and turning on his rough bed.

Rory Blain said: "I'd like to git that hellion, Chet Wayne. Thet jigger gits in my hair! He turned up jest as we were gittin' Doc Harper out o' his house."

"Did he see yuh?"

"I don't see how he could. It was pretty dark. We saw him walk around the blamed house first. I threw him some slugs but I reckon the light was bad."

Luke Starn said thoughtfully: "I figger we've got to get rid o' thet hombre. Tom Hudson made a bad play in acceptin' thet jigger as deputy. Now I reckon we ought to have a new deputy — a feller we kin trust!"

Doc Harper walked on steadily through the night, and he thought there was more illumination. He fancied the moon was ready to rise.

He had covered four miles, he reckoned, when he heard the sound of hoof-beats in the night. He stopped, wondered who might be ridin' out.

Inside ten minutes he located the riders. The sound of hoof-beats carried a long way. Then he shouted.

He was picked up by some men from Laredo who had left town to look for the Doc.

But Doc Harper kept doggedly silent. He listened to the remarks that were flung around and realized the men knew he had been kidnapped. Then he heard one man shout:

"Chet Wayne says one o' them jiggers was Rory Blain. That right, Doc?"

"Jest get me home!" grated Doc Harper. "An' don't ask questions I cain't answer."

"Wal, doggone me!"

And Doc Harper was thoughtful as

he rode back on a horse belonging to a rancher friend. He had to double-up, but his sparse frame could have made little load for the big horse. Eventually the party rode into town. Doc Harper went straight to his house. Hardly a minute elapsed and then Chet Wayne and Tom Hudson came along.

"What was Rory Blain up to, Doc?" asked Chet quietly.

The Doc stroked his white moustache nervously.

"Did I say one of those jiggers was Rory Blain?"

"His hat was found. An old hombre saw the two hosses cantering by when the hat fell. It was Rory Blain's hat."

"Yuh could be making a mistake!" snapped Doc Harper. "Aw, great snakes, jest let me have some rest. I'm not as young as I used to be."

"Those galoots must ha' had some good reason for hustling yuh away," countered Chet.

"Maybe they had. Yeah. Well, Deputy, I got nothin' to say for the moment.

Maybe I got to do some thinkin'. I figger the whole thing can keep."

"They've been threatenin' yuh," said Chet shrewdly.

Doc Harper nodded.

"Yeah. Now git. An' I didn't say Rory Blain was one of those jiggers."

The men turned to the door.

"Yuh'll be sayin' nothin' ever happened to yuh before long," said Chet grimly. "All right, Doc. I can guess you don't want to talk. An' I can guess why. Maybe yuh're right. Maybe this can keep."

Sheriff Tom Hudson was glad to get out of the Doc's house without having to commit himself.

The two lawmen went back to the office. For the moment the dead border breed in the yard was forgotten. His disposal could wait.

Chet Wayne paced the office, disgruntled.

"Rory Blain was tangled in that play. That jigger ought to be rounded up."

"The Doc has to make a charge," said Tom Hudson slowly. "I don't see how we kin prove anythin' iffen the Doc won't make a charge."

"All right!" Chet snapped the words. "But I don't like it. And another thing, there's too much lawless shoo-shaying around goin' on in this town. Some jiggers are gitting away with too much."

Chet Wayne went out later and took himself along to the Gold Nugget saloon. He was a moderate drinking man, but liked the conviviality of his fellow men as much as the next hombre.

He met up with Walt Carr, the rancher, who was in town that night, and they spent some time talking about the Blains, Doc Harper and Tom Hudson.

"What this town needs is a new sheriff," said Walt Carr. "Somethin' has changed Tom. He used to be a fast-mover, but now he don't seem to bother much."

A man called Dave Guarde, whom most men in the saloon knew to be the owner of a bonanza ten miles out of Laredo, pushed through the batwings and came up to the bar. Spotting Chet Wayne, he said loudly:

"Howdy, Deputy! I heerd yuh bin having trouble with some bad men. Wal, it ain't nothin' to what I got jest some hours ago."

"Somethin' wrong? Anything I can do?" asked Chet.

"Wal, maybe. I bin robbed. I chartered a Concord to take out a consignment o' gold chips, an' the stage was shot up an' the gold lifted. Hell, this town is gettin' worse! I chartered the stage because I figgered it was fast. I had two jiggers with rifles ride alongside the driver. Durn me, it cost almost as much in pay to get that gold movin'. But some blamed robbers got it instead o' the bank!"

"What about yore men? Did they see the robbers?" asked Chet swiftly.

"Maybe they did. But it didn't do 'em any good because my men on that stage are all dead now!"

4

CHET WAYNE balanced on the balls of his feet, his thumbs hooked into his gun-belt, his Stetson pushed back slightly, revealing the grim expression on his face.

The hubbub in the Gold Nugget had died to a murmur upon Dave Guarde's statement. The men who patronized the saloon were mostly men of some solid worth in the town and while the stolen gold was not their loss, the death of men killed while doing a job angered them.

"Yuh reported this to the sheriff?" asked one man.

Dave Guarde's full-fleshed face looked momentarily sardonic.

"Would thet do any good?" he asked.

One man guffawed, and some others made growling noises. Nothing else was said about Tom Hudson, although Walt

Carr and another rancher shot curious glances at Chet Wayne.

"Where the heck did this holdup start?" asked Chet abruptly.

"Seven miles out along the Joshua Trail. I wanted the consignment in Abilene fast."

"Wasn't the consignment kept secret?"

"Yeah. Shore. But them jiggers were waitin' for the Concord. I figger they've been watchin' me."

"Maybe they saw the Concord roll into yore mine," said Chet reflectively.

"Could be. Wal, they got my gold."

"How did yuh learn about the holdup?"

"Wal, Deputy, iffen it will do any good I don't mind yore questions. I got kinda restless about thet stage an' I rode out along the trail later. Jest kinda wanted to see the wheel marks. I rode on an' was figgerin' everything was all right, when hell, I saw them hands o' mine lyin' in their own blood."

"An' the stage?"

"Those jiggers had taken it."

"Did yuh track the wheel marks?"

"Yeah. Rode 'bout two miles an' got near the foothills. Then I found the Concord. Them durned bandits had shifted the gold. I had a good looksee at the signs around. I figure they had some pack hosses waitin' an' they'd driven the stage up to meet the pack hosses. Plenty o' sign o' hosses hoofs. An' the stage was abandoned."

"How long ago was all this, Mister Guarde?"

"About maybe two hours ago."

"Goldarn it, I reckon I was asleep right then!" exclaimed Chet.

There was a laugh from one man.

"Was Sheriff Hudson asleep, Deputy?"

"I don't know where he was," said Chet harshly.

"I didn't ride into town right away," explained Dave Guarde, "because I had plenty to do. I figger I wasted some time trackin' the Concord. Then I got back to the mine and raged around. I thought maybe some o' them hands were in cahoots with the bandits, but I don't

74

know. Then I rode over here — an' thet's ten miles!"

Chet paced restlessly.

"Those durned owl-hoots could be anywhere with thet gold by now! All right, Mister Guarde, come on over an' talk to the sheriff. He's in the office, I think."

The two men walked out, heels rapping sharply on the boards. They crossed the dusty road and made for the sheriff's office.

Chet was half-way to the building when the idea struck him. He began to connect up events.

The dead breed in the yard behind the office hardly mattered, except for the fact that someone had induced the man to attempt the killing.

Chet thought that was a pretty sound conclusion. But there were other ideas circulating slowly in his mind.

Doc Harper had been abducted and then found unharmed. He had a strange reluctance to talk, but it was not difficult to guess at his reasons. Then it seemed certain that Rory Blain was one of the hombres who had hustled the Doc away.

Some queer hunch in Chet's mind prompted the conclusion that there was some connection between the stealing of Dave Guarde's gold and the brief kidnapping of Doc Harper.

Chet turned to the gold mine owner. "Yuh go on over to see Tom Hudson. I got an idea I want to try out. Tell Tom Hudson everythin'."

"Yeah. Maybe I'm wastin' my blamed time!" said the other grimly.

Chet strode away and walked the length of the dusty main street. There was no time limit for the saloons, and many of them were still doing a roaring trade.

But Chet Wayne had no time for these observations. Swiftly, he approached Doc Harper's pleasant little home on the outskirts of the town.

Some minutes later he was inside the house, standing close to a stone fireplace, his feet on Indian rugs.

"Rory Blain was the rannigan who

hustled yuh away. That right, Doc?"

"I don't think I said so, Mister Deputy."

"All right," said Chet unsmilingly. "I figger I can prove that without yore statement. But I'd shore like to know where those catamounts took yuh."

Doc Harper stroked his white moustache.

"There ain't no use pestering me, young feller. I can't tell you anythin'. Yuh ought to understand. I'm an old man an' I've seen more than my share o' stiffs, but I've no hankerin' to join them on boothill just now."

"Like that, is it?"

"I guess so. I'd like to help" — for a moment the Doc almost choked with anger — "but those hellions ha' got me tangled in my own loop!"

Chet tried another angle.

"Yuh don't know that Dave Guarde had a stage held up an' a consignment o' gold lifted. Happened jest a few hours ago. Some guards got killed."

Doc Harper jerked his head.

"Stage! Guards!"

"Yeah. I jest got the story."

Chet watched as the doctor paced around the room. In his tweed suit, with the heavy gold watch-chain across the vest, the little man appeared to be seriously perturbed.

"Them durned hellions! Ought to be strung up!" He stared at Chet, appeared almost to blurt out some remark and then changed his mind with an effort.

"This is a lawless town, Doc. We've got to work together to rout out these killers."

"Were the guards on the stage killed?"

"Yeah, according to the gold mine owner. Seems like a gang behind it." Chet paused and added quietly: "I wonder if any o' those hellions got hurt in the shootin'?"

Doc Harper ground one fist into the palm of his other hand. He glared at the floor.

"One o' them outlaws did get hurt!" he blurted out.

Chet nodded.

"Yuh were hustled out to attend the jigger. Where did yuh go, Doc? Who did yuh see? Apart from Rory Blain?"

"Why don't yuh tackle thet young rannigan?" breathed the other.

"That's a pleasure to come to!" snapped Chet. "Don't think I'm lettin' up on him. All right, Doc, who did you see? I reckon yuh can tell me a lot."

"I can see myself up on boothill!" roared Doc Harper. "With a bellyful o' slugs! An' I reckon I won't be hackin' them out myself!" He kept on roaring, like a little man yelling his defiance. "Sure that wild fool Rory Blain took me out! And I had to fix up a hellion who had some rifle slug in his carcass! By thunder, how he cursed! How he was a-goin' to shoot some stage guard as soon as he got better! And I had to patch this owl-hoot so that he could go after some damned stage guard!"

"The feller must ha' been crazy," snapped Chet. "The men workin' for Dave Guarde were all killed. Who was this man yuh patched up, Doc?"

Doc Harper took a deep breath.

"Look, Deputy, I'm just like any other hombre. I don't want to die with blood spilling out o' my belly. So I'm goin' to tell yuh what I know as long as yuh keep it to yoreself. Understand? Yuh got to promise not to tell Sheriff Hudson or anyone else anything I tell yuh!"

"All right. That suits me," said Chet grimly. "Anythin' that will let me git to grips with those hombres suits me."

"All right, Deputy. Wal, I was taken to a shack set up in the foothills near Snake's Hole — one o' those ruined mine workings. Rory Blain an' a hombre name o' Mulaney took me up. Then we met Luke Starn, and inside the shack was a shot-up gink by the name o' Daniel Grig. That's the gent who cursed about killin' a stage guard. Luke Starn stopped his talk, and I figure I heard too much. Anyway, I had to take rifle slugs out of this jigger."

"That all?"

"Ain't it enough? I was told to keep my trap shut an' walk back to town. Lucky fer me I got picked up. I don't like walkin' all those miles at my age!"

"They let you go?" Chet paced slowly.

"Yeah, an' I was told if I squawked, they'd fill me full of lead. Now for Gawd's sake, keep this to yoreself, Deputy!"

"I will," assented Chet. "It's enough for me to work on. I'm ridin' out tonight."

"Where yuh headin'?"

"I figger to pick up that Dan Grig an' make him talk," said Chet grimly. "If I can make that hombre talk, I've got somethin' on Rory Blain, Luke Starn and his hired side-kick Mulaney."

And with that the deputy sheriff of Laredo let himself out of the neat little house.

He left behind a worried old man who promptly bolted the door and went to a locker where some guns were kept.

Doc Harper brought out a Colt gun. He loaded it and sought out a gunbelt. He strapped the belt on and holstered the gun. Then he stared at a rifle on the wall. He had not used it for some time, but he thought this was an emergency that justified loading the Winchester and having it lay by in readiness.

Chet Wayne strode back to the livery where his horse was stabled. Blackie had still not gained sufficient rest from the desert trek, and he did not intend to use the great animal yet.

Chet slipped the saddle on to the horse he had used later that evening. He rode out of the livery. He did not meet Sheriff Tom Hudson. He thought maybe Dave Guarde was still repeating his account of his lost gold and dead hands.

Doc Harper's yarn had cinched a few points in his mind. He could visualize many more.

The news about Luke Starn gave him some grim satisfaction. He had suspected the man was lawless. Although it was too early to obtain concrete proof, it seemed Luke Starn was bossing a gang of bandits. Rory Blain was in with him, too. The wild Blain blood was showing up again. Then there was Mulaney and Dan Grig. The fact that the last-named man had been wounded in a fight with some stage guards was significant. There had been only one stage holdup in the territory that day and it could only be the one Dave Guarde had chartered to transport his gold.

Obtaining the sort of proof that would convict these lawless men would not be easy. But to Chet it seemed that the wounded Dan Grig was a key man. If he could be picked up and made to talk before witnesses or, better still, if he could be induced to make a statement and sign it, a first-class coup might be had.

Chet had promised to keep his news to himself. In a queer way, this was a relief. Inwardly, he wanted to keep this news from Tom Hudson. It was a disturbing idea and he could not analyse it.

He cantered the horse out of the town, keeping to some side-streets. He felt that it was better to avoid any townsfolk. Some of the men, recently excited about Doc Harper's mysterious hijacking, might ask awkward questions.

Chet Wayne just wanted to indulge in a little lone-wolf work. He would see what results could be obtained.

As the night air out on the semi-arid land enfolded him, his thoughts did turn to Jane Blain. She was in an unpleasant position because of her wild brothers. Chet felt kind of bitter about the setup. His friendship with Jane had never had a chance. He had been forced to hunt down one brother; now he was on the trail of the other hot-head buckeroo.

If Rory went the same way as Bernard, Jane would find life on the Double X difficult. A girl could not cope with the work on the hard-living spread. And Jane would hate the very man who would give a lot to help her!

Chet began thinking about Doc Harper's statements. The shack was over by Snake's Hole apparently. He thought he knew the place. It was about seven miles out, amid a lot of rocky wasteland and silvery cholla cactus.

He was armed for the ride. Two Colts hung low in shiny leather holsters. Although Chet never made many bones about it, he could scoop those guns out faster than many men this side of the border.

For the first part of the ride he allowed the horse full lope. The sure-footed animal avoided the jack rabbit holes and the clumps of prickly pear. The moon was gleaming somewhere low on the horizon; there would be more light later. Chet Wayne was not sure if he wanted a lot of moonlight. It would not make much difference whether he wanted it or not; Old Man Moon would be there!

Snake's Hole was a rocky basin just before the broken country. This was where the land became mostly sand and shale, homes only for the rattler and the cholla cactus, the bristly thickets of prickly pear and the skeleton-like ocotillo. The flatter parts of the semi-arid land were deceptive and most of the grass was bunch grass which, even when withered, was just as nutritious for longhorns as corn. But up in the foothills sand and shale, cactus and rattler held sway.

Chet Wayne slowed the horse when he judged he was near to the broken country. For one thing fast riding at night was dangerous. And for another, hoofbeats carried a long way in the night. He would let the cayuse carry him with lighter progress. In any case, he had to peer through the night for sign of the derelict cabin.

The horse plodded along slowly. Chet leaned on the saddle-horn, stared around keenly. The gaunt shapes of piled-up volcanic rocks, worn by thousands of years of rain and sand-filled winds, moved past him — or seemed to!

There was a ghostly silence around this wasteland.

He was searching for the cabin, and he knew he would find it. He had not been around this neck of the land for some time, but he remembered passing a derelict mine from a distance on one ride.

He came upon the shack slowly. He first spotted it through the wan light when he was about a hundred yards from it. He at once dismounted and paused with the horse, his hand over its nostrils in case it scented other hidden horses and whinnied.

He led the horse to a rocky nook between some sandstone boulders and hitched the reins to a protuberance. He took out a large red handkerchief from a shirt pocket and tore strips off it. He tied these strips around his spurs. This would prevent any jingling sound which might be picked up by alert ears.

Chet did not know what he would find. The man called Dan Grig obviously should still be in the shack.

A man who had been recently shot up could not ride a horse. But the others might have left him.

In a sense Chet hoped to find that state of affairs. Unless he was exceptionally lucky, he could not expect to get the drop on the other three hardy hombres. He might, of course, get the drop on them — but bringing the men in to Laredo would be pretty ticklish.

If he got the chance, he would take it. At the moment, a bit of investigating was required.

He came forward with soft deliberate strides. His boots fell on sand. Before he got close to the shack, there was a stretch of shale. He walked across it carefully, glad that he did not disturb one loose stone.

At closer inspection, there was a light in the cabin. The one window was shuttered, but faint chinks of light escaped from some cracks. That meant someone was inside.

He paused, loosened a Colt from one holster and went forward, gun in hand.

He got close to the shack wall and stood still, beside the shuttered window, listening.

At first he heard little or nothing of any significance. Then he heard the clumsy clump of footsteps. Someone was walking across the wooden floor.

Chet Wayne was in no great hurry. He maintained a listening attitude for some time and a few points became clear.

He heard a voice, which was a growling reply to a muttered moan.

There was a distinct pause before the sound of a voice was heard again. Once more it was the growling tones of a man who is slightly disgruntled.

Chet figured there was only one man in the cabin besides Dan Grig. He was willing to stake a lot on that.

It was disappointing in one way, and yet easier in another. Of course, he should have brought out a posse to this cabin; but that was impossible because he had promised Doc Harper to keep the information to himself.

Chet sidled around to the shack door. He wondered if it was barred from the inside. Probably it was.

He paused grimly. This was where the play could take the right turn or the wrong one.

It had to take the right trail!

He wanted the man named Dan Grig. He had a hunch he could make him talk.

Chet stared at the door for a second. For the second time he wondered if it was barred on the inside. If it was not, the best plan was to burst into the cabin, hogleg pretty prominent!

But the chances were the door was locked or barred. To try it would reveal his presence.

A sudden thought occurred to Chet Wayne.

Silently, he sidled away from the cabin. He trod warily over loose shale and congratulated himself upon his noiseless progress. He came up to the rising heap of rock which constituted the bluff.

He was looking for horses or a horse.

The man in the cabin with Grig must have his horse corralled somewhere. He would not be out here in the wastelands without a cayuse.

Chet soon found the makeshift corral. There was a cleft in the bluff and two horses were stabled there, with two rough planks stretched across to serve as a barrier.

Chet had to take the chance of the critturs greeting his approach with sounds. Quickly, he removed the planks. Then he led the two animals out, holding them by their manes. The horses were unsaddled, proving they were stabled for the night.

Chet led the animals over to the cabin. There was nothing he could do to prevent their slow clop-clop of hoof-beats. But from the improvised corral to the shack was only a matter of seconds, and it did not matter if the men in the cabin heard the horses moving.

In fact that was just what Chet Wayne wanted!

He simply wanted the man with Grig to think the horses had strayed. That would get him out of the cabin! The door would be opened, cross-bar or not!

Chet got the horses right up to the shack door, and then he slipped around the corner.

He had two guns out now. He gave a glance around the edge of the shack. The horses were nosing against the cabin! They were moving slowly and would probably wander inside a minute.

Then Chet heard the sounds of clumping boots inside the shack.

He heard the rasp of a bar being lifted, and he smiled thinly. He had been right. The door had been barred. Trying to open it would have been a bad move.

He wondered who was inside the shack. Was it Rory Blain? Or Luke Starn? Or maybe the man called Mulaney?

Suddenly he heard an oath; then grating sounds as a man lurched after two startled horses. Boots slithered against loose shale. Unlike Chet Wayne, the man had no reason to move silently!

Chet came round the edge of the shack. Two guns poked around first. Then he followed up.

The hombre grappling with the horses was not Rory Blain, he knew in an instant. And it was not Luke Starn. Even in the poor, wan light he could discern that. So the man was Mulaney? One of the many Irish desperadoes, no doubt.

It was a grim swift moment when Chet rasped:

"Stick 'em up, hombre!"

The man had the courage of a fool. Or maybe he was a hell-bent rannigan who hated being tricked.

Mulaney turned as if to look at the other man. His hands were wavering in a motion that could be anything from staying put to hoisting sky-high!

Chet gave him the benefit of the doubt for just two seconds too long!

Mulaney wheeled and then his hands sank to holsters. He was flashing hands desperately to hoglegs. It was an incredible clawing motion that might have beaten anyone but another swift gunslinger.

Even so Colts roared simultaneously — or nearly so! Chet was only a split second ahead of the outlaw. The bark of guns hid that fraction of time.

But the slugs that tore out from orange flame bit into Mulaney with terrible force. He actually commenced his death stagger as he had fired. The consequence was his guns were unsighted. The Colts roared all right, but the lead sang around Chet's new Stetson.

Slugs found Mulaney. Under the impact, he staggered, dropping one gun and clutching at his dirty shirt-front.

Chet watched the man's legs buckle and, with a contorted expression, he fell forward. He clawed at the sand for a moment and then, with a terrible shudder, lay still.

Chet Wayne turned unsmiling blue eyes towards the shack entrance.

He did not doubt Dan Grig had heard the shooting. The man might conceivably have a gun.

No one else would have heard the shots. There was nothing but wasteland for miles. It was a good bet that Rory Blain and Luke Starn had ridden off to other destinations.

There was the question of the stolen gold, for instance. It would have to be cached or sold immediately. Some of the men would have to attend to that job.

Chet strode into the cabin, slowly at first and then with a quicker movement when he saw the man on the bunk cursing and striving to sit up.

"Yuh're Dan Grig!" snapped Chet. "I figger yuh been wounded while robbing Dave Guarde of his gold consignment. Yuh're under arrest. Yuh know me. I'm Deputy Wayne."

The man had no gun. But he looked pretty exhausted. Chet realized there was a problem in getting the hombre to Laredo. If the man died on his hands, he would not be much good as a witness against Luke Starn and Rory Blain!

5

JANE BLAIN watched the two men as they sprawled in the wood-framed easy chairs. The living-room of the ranch-house was big enough, but these two seemed to fill it. They both looked in reckless good spirits. Luke Starn held his glass of whisky as if amused and triumphant. His dark eyes followed Jane's slim form as she moved slowly around the room, gathering her needle-work from a cabinet and placing it near her favourite chair.

She was attractive and on this occasion completely feminine in a floral gingham dress. Her long brown hair coiled nicely at the back of her head. Jane did not always wear plaid shirt and levis.

Rory Blain noticed Luke Starn's gaze. The young buckeroo had been laughing and talking gustily, often slipping some significant boasts into his speech when Jane was in another room. Now he snickered and raised his glass.

"Hyar's to you two! Say, when the heck's it gonna be?"

"Jane don't want to be rushed," said Luke Starn smoothly, his knowledge of women asserting itself. "But I reckon we kin make a date with the preacher 'most any time now. That so, Jane?"

There was some mocking in the flung question.

Jane did not answer. She bent over her needle-work.

"I reckon it's right and proper that a lone woman should be married," said Rory Blain. He said it quickly, as if convincing himself.

"This is a hard territory," said Luke Starn blandly. "A gal ought to know she needs the right sort of galoot to look after her. Ain't thet right, you two?"

Still Jane did not answer. Rory Blain muttered something.

Luke Starn set down his glass with a

spasm of irritation. Suddenly he reached out and grabbed at Jane's hand.

"Why don't yuh answer?"

"I've nothin' to say," she said quietly.

"Maybe yuh'd like to be married tomorrow!" he sneered.

She glanced at him with scorn. He noticed it.

"Why you little skirt, I've half a mind to ride yuh over to Laredo now an' hustle out the preacher! I'd make that sky-pilot marry us tonight!"

"That's ridiculous!" she breathed.

"Takes the haughty look out o' yore face, don't it?" he sneered.

"I — I — can't marry you!" she flung at him.

He flushed into immediate anger. His dark, saturnine face set and his eyes flickered unpleasantly.

"By thunder, yuh will marry me an' when I say! Yuh know that durned well. I reckon a hombre like me needs a wife — an upstanding, respectable sort o' woman an' not those honky-tonk gals! I'm goin' to be a big man

99

in Laredo. Yuh're a little fool not to realize that."

"Perhaps I am a fool — but — I don't love you!" She clenched her hands, stared unseeingly at him.

"Thet don't matter a damn!" he snarled. "Yuh'll be my wife or I'll sell this durned ranch over yore head. Rory owes me money — a lot o' money! Thet ain't all. There was a killin' in Abilene one night a month ago. A jigger shot up a harmless cuss in a bar an' then dashed out for his hoss an' beat it. That jigger was Rory, an' the Town Marshal would shore like to know about him, seeing no gink in the bar got a look at him, the shooting happened so fast!"

"Yuh'll git yore damned money when I get my share o' the — " Rory Blain stopped and twisted his lip in a sneer. "Yuh know what I mean."

Jane gave her brother a sharp glance. She was no fool and she realized now that Rory was engaged on some lawless exploit with Luke Starn.

"Maybe I'll git the money," said Luke

Starn. "An' I reckon to git the gal. Yeah, a respectable wife makes her husband seem respectable! Guess that's what I want!"

Jane blazed at him.

"Oh, you're hounding me! You know I hate you! Why don't you leave me alone! You've got Rory in your power — why do you want me?"

He was a man of swift, ugly anger. With two strides he was over to her and had grasped both her hands and hauled her up.

"I've told yuh why I want yuh! A man needs to put on a good front if he figgers to become a power in a town. I reckon I'll be the leadin' citizen of this burg pretty soon. So I guess a galoot needs a respectable gal for a wife."

"You could find your type of woman in the saloons of Laredo!" she flung at him.

She tried to free her hands, but he held her grimly.

"By thunder, yuh'll be my wife!" he breathed. "An' then I'll tame yuh."

"Let go of me!"

He tried to draw her closer. She managed to free one of her hands, and she whipped it furiously to his cheek.

The smack sounded loud in the ranch-house. Luke Starn stared with glinting eyes at the girl. Rory Blain shifted uneasily, a disgruntled expression upon his face.

"By Gawd, thet settles it!" Luke Starn became blazing with anger. "We're a-goin' over to Laredo now! Rory — git a hoss ready for yore sister, We're goin' to be married, right an' proper — tonight!"

"Yuh don't have to rush Jane off her feet," growled Rory.

Luke Starn swung back to the girl.

"She's a-comin' of her own free will. That right, Jane? Yuh want to marry me — ain't that right? Yuh don't want Rory in the hoose-gow at Abilene!"

"I — I — don't know!" choked the girl.

"Speak to her, Rory!" jeered Luke Starn. "Tell her what she's got to do!"

Rory Blain hung his head low, chin

sinking to his chest. Then he jerked his head upwards.

"Jane — yuh heard what he said! Yuh ain't got nuthin' to be scared of. Luke's goin' to be a big man in this town. Durn it, yuh'll have everythin' yuh want if yuh're his wife!"

"We've gone over all this before!" burst out Jane.

Rory's face hardened.

"Shore. An' yuh promised to marry Luke Starn."

"To help you to save you from a hangnoose!"

Luke Starn gestured angrily.

"That still stands. Git the hosses. Go ahead, Rory. Yuh got nothin' to lose when yuh work with me!"

Rory Blain moved towards the door and then stared back at the other man.

"All right. We'll ride. Guess yuh won't rest until the knot's tied. Wal, if yuh stop a slug after Jane marries yuh, she'll be yore widow an' entitled to any property yuh leave. I figger that's a good point."

The gambler desperado broke into a guffaw.

"Hell, yuh don't reckon to deal me that slug, do yuh? You an' me got big things to do together. I've got the brains and you've got the brawn. Yuh can forget the slug angle."

"I never figgered to deal a pardner a slug," said Rory Blain quickly.

"Wal, that's fine. Glad to hear it."

"But yuh know there'll be Colt slugs flyin' pretty soon. A hombre jest takes his chance. That's what I meant."

"Shore, shore! Wal, let's git goin'. By thunder, I want to get on with this. We'll ride over an' rout out that sky-pilot. By hell, it ain't every day a man gits married! We'll have some drinks on this tonight. Shore, I got some pals in Laredo saloons an' I reckon they'd be mighty glad to throw a party."

"D'yuh figger Doc Harper will keep his trap shut?"

"Yeah! What do you think? Shore. He's a Doc, but he cain't patch himself up if he's dead."

Luke Starn broke into a rich chuckle at his joke. He had recovered his temper somewhat. But his hard mind had gripped one domineering thought.

He was determined to ride Jane into town and marry her.

It was surprising, but the man was sincere when he spoke of acquiring a wife with a respectable status. Laredo was fifty per cent lawless; but just as many folks worked hard at keeping law and justice. Luke Starn knew he would have to deal with the law-loving if he wanted to be a powerful man in the town. If he wanted to buy and sell, acquire more property, he would have to deal with the law-abiding-as well as keep Tom Hudson in his power and control a gang of hired owl-hoots!

All this meant building up a status in the town. He planned to keep his lawless activities under cover. At the least he figured if he had the sheriff in his power, he could make it difficult for proof of his nefarious doings to be levelled against him.

To Luke Starn's ruthless mind, Jane would make an ideal background for an important man. He had spent money on the painted dance-hall women, but he was not taking one of them for a wife.

In quick time Rory Blain had the three horses ready outside the ranch-house.

Jane was very quiet. She was pale, dry-eyed and controlled. Her appearance did not show the whirl of thoughts in her mind.

For a long time she had defended her wild brothers against all criticism although she knew in her heart they were wasters. Bernard was dead, killed by Chet Wayne. Now Rory was under the thumb of Luke Starn. She just had to help Rory. But she hardly knew what course to take.

One thing was certain — Luke Starn was ruthless enough to carry out his threat of handing Rory over to the Town Marshal at Abilene. How he would do it, she did not know — probably by some trickery when Rory was least suspecting it. But the threat was real.

Arguments seemed futile. She was still thinking her way around her problems when she found herself being assisted to her saddled horse. Before she realized what was happening, she was sitting side-saddle. Rory brought out a shawl for her and she took it mechanically. She was wearing a dress that made sitting astride the horse impossible.

"Let's git!" said Luke Starn triumphantly.

Jane felt her horse wheel with the other two. The mounts headed for the open gate in the ranch yard fencing. The ranch-house soon lay behind, the door locked and the lamp extinguished. Rory Blain had seen to those essential chores while Jane's mind had swirled.

They were heading across the semi-arid range, with hoofs beating a tattoo that raised dust and the faint aroma of sage. Rory Blain was silent, but Luke Starn was in a reckless mood. He began

107

to sing a wild song in a deep baritone. For an unpleasant person, he had a curiously good voice.

"I'm longing for the gal, who'll sure marry me — " He broke off and roared: "Hey, Rory! Why the blazes don't yuh sing? Ain't yuh had enough likker?"

"I'm thinkin' o' thet blamed deputy," lied Rory.

"Him? Haw! Haw! Guess we can take care of that hombre most any old time! C'mon, I want to hear yuh sing!"

Rory Blain joined in, and if his voice was not as loud as the other man's, it was because he had a different role that night. He was a rough-living buckeroo, but deep down he knew that it was because of his fool exploits that Jane was due to marry this man.

After a while, what with the fast ride and Luke Starn's boisterous songs, he forgot his scruples. Marrying Jane off to Luke Starn was probably the best way out. And it kept him out of the Law's hands.

They entered the outskirts of Laredo

but did not gallop down the main stem. Instead, Luke Starn wheeled down the straggling outskirts of the community, thundering by some motley shacks and pole corrals. Jane's horse was wedged between the two. She had no alternative but to go with the others.

Luke Starn evidently had certain ideas in his mind. He knew where the preacher's house lay.

He began to boast, now that his songs had died away.

"This sky-pilot will do anythin' I say. I reckon gold talks." He jerked his head to Rory. "You'll learn that pretty soon. Gold talks."

Luke Starn suddenly reined in beside an unlighted house set back from the road and wedged between a barber's shop and a gunsmith's store.

"Git yore boots to ground. This is the place."

They dismounted. No sooner had Jane slid to the dusty road than Luke Starn took her arm. With his other hand he completed looping his reins to a hitching rail. Then he threw the reins of Jane's horse over the tie-rail. He smiled into her face.

"Yuh don't have to be scared, honey. In no time you'll be Mrs. Starn! A lot o' wimmen in this town would figure that a great idea!"

But there was menace in his mocking words, and Jane sensed it. He was telling her, in his sardonic way, that resistance would bring more grief to the Double X.

Rory Blain looked around at the area where pale moonlight threw a wan illumination.

"Let's git in," he muttered.

Horses hitched to the tie-rail, they moved towards the unlighted house.

Luke Starn knocked, a low but decisive tap on an iron knocker. They waited.

A lamp slowly glowed from a window and then moved away as if someone was carrying it. A few moments later the front door opened cautiously.

The man behind the door was clad in

tight black trousers and white shirt. He seemed pretty mussed up, as if he had been sleeping or lying down. His first words indicated that he was not in too good a temper.

"What d'yuh want this time o' night?"

"Take a good look, Simister!" snarled Luke Starn. "Yuh know me. We're comin' in. You've got work to do, hombre."

Carl Simister was a preacher, but happily for the folks of Laredo not the only one in town. He was, however, the only preacher who had a crooked streak.

The man stood to one side, and the party moved forward. Carl Simister wore a sickly smile. He had already guessed the nature of the setup.

"We're plannin' on a wedding," said Luke Starn.

"Tonight?"

"Yeah. Why not?"

"Ain't usual, that's all."

"You'll get paid. Yuh know that."

"Shore, that's all right with me," said the preacher quickly. "Yuh got some witnesses?"

"There's Rory Blain — " began Luke Starn.

"He's the gal's brother, ain't he?" broke in Carl Simister. "He's got to give her away. I reckon yuh need another witness, Mister Starn. Yuh need a signature."

Luke Starn wheeled on Rory Blain.

"Damblast this! Go round up some galoot. Get some jigger who's agreeable, but I don't want some low hombre. Git a man who folks respects. An' make it fast!"

"Aw, quit shoutin'," said Rory irritably. "I'll git some feller. You got pals. How about the sheriff? He's got plenty o' status in this burg!"

Luke Starn gave a laugh.

"That's an idea! Yuh couldn't think up a better man than Tom Hudson. See if yuh can git him — but watch out for thet blamed deputy!"

Rory Blain paused to mutter angrily:

112

"Thet galoot better not git in my way. I got a hogleg that's itching to throw lead at thet jigger!"

Jane heard the sour boast with a choking sensation inside her. True, she felt she could not forgive Chet Wayne for hunting down and killing Bernard, but nevertheless she hated the thought that there might be bloodshed between Chet and Rory.

She felt dazed with it all. She could not think properly. Why must there be so much hatred and fighting?

And then Rory left. He unhitched his horse and rowelled it into a canter. His dark shape disappeared down the street. He was away in search of Sheriff Tom Hudson.

Jane was alone with a man she feared and another who filled her with disgust.

6

CHET WAYNE was riding back at full lope to Laredo. He hunched low in the saddle to lessen his wind resistance. He used his spur rowels infrequently. The cayuse was still fresh and moving nicely.

He was alone. He had come to the conclusion that it was impossible to ride Dan Grig back to Laredo without having the fellow die on his hands. As a witness he would be no good on boothill!

Chet realized he should have tried to take Mulaney prisoner; but, of course, there had been little choice. The outlaw had gone for his gun. Chet had had to beat the man on the draw. The question had been one of survival.

Chet figured to get Sheriff Tom Hudson spurred into some activity. If the sheriff would not ride out that night to take a deposition from Dan Grig supposing they could get one then Chet intended to round up some reputable men and suggest a vigilante committee be formed.

The way he saw it, Dan Grig could clinch the case against Luke Starn and Rory Blain. He had Rory Blain's hat to prove the man had kidnapped Doc Harper. If a deposition could be got from Dan Grig, Doc Harper might add his evidence. This way Luke Starn and Rory Blain could be convicted of murder. Until they were caught, they would be branded as outlaws.

There was some grim satisfaction in lining up these thoughts. With some luck the dead stage guards would be avenged. What was more, justice would be carried out. A case would be built up and Judge Tarrant preside. The lawless who had swarmed into Laredo of late would be warned.

Chet Wayne thundered into the town, making good speed through the night. The moon was now throwing pale light over the outer, unlighted streets. When he came to the main stem he encountered the floods of yellow light emanating from the noisy saloons. They were still going full blast.

He reined the horse to a canter as he approached the sheriff's office. Shadows lay around the building as he vaulted from the saddle and threw a hitch over a tie-rail.

He wondered if Tom Hudson would be inside the office. The shutters were clamped over the windows. Probably Dave Guarde had taken himself back to the Gold Nugget or maybe the man had ridden back home to his bonanza.

Chet walked towards the boardwalk and then halted in the shadow of a heavy post as the door of the building opened.

Two men walked out. Instinctively, Chet Wayne slid closer to the heavy wooden post and lay concealed.

He had recognized Sheriff Tom Hudson. The other figure was no other than Rory Blain!

116

The two men were exchanging low words as they walked out. Tom Hudson used a very disgruntled tone.

"I don't like this chore, I tell yuh!"

"Luke Starn wants yuh!" sneered Rory Blain. "He's the boss, ain't he?"

"Yuh marrying yore sister to thet skunk — " Tom Hudson almost choked.

"Tell Luke Starn he's a skunk to his face!" snapped Rory Blain. "C'mon. My hoss is around in the alley."

Behind the big supporting post, Chet stiffened. His hands dropped to twin Colts. But he did not draw.

He had heard a few startling words. And a swift hunch struck him. These two men were departing on some mission.

Chet could have stepped out and arrested Rory Blain on a charge of kidnapping Doc Harper. If Rory had gone for his hardware, it would have been a question of gun-speed.

Chet Wayne was not worried about his speed with a Colt. He figured he could beat the quickest gun-slingers this side of the border.

He wanted to learn more.

There was some grim significance in that Tom Hudson was consorting with Rory Blain. But worse than that, to Chet's tensed mind, was the hint that Jane was being married to Luke Starn.

Chet did not understand everything clearly. But he remembered the occasion he had found Luke Starn holding Jane in his arms. The memory rankled even now. Was it possible that Jane had agreed to marry the gambler desperado?

Surely Jane was not so blind as that? What, then, was the answer?

With these questions in his mind, Chet Wayne moved slowly away from the post.

The two men had rounded a corner just past the sheriff's office. As Chet stepped forward slowly, still in the shadows, a horse cantered out of the alley, with a sudden rataplan of hoof-beats. The animal carried two men.

118

Chet darted back to his own horse. He wanted to follow Tom Hudson and Rory Blain and see just what sort of play was going on.

He had little idea how far the two would be riding, but it did strike him that the distance could not be very great or Tom Hudson would have saddled a horse for himself. Therefore the two men were bound for only a short ride.

Chet gained his saddle swiftly. When the two men had left the office they had evidently not noticed the dim shape of the horse. Or probably the sight of a cayuse hitched to a rail meant nothing to them.

His eyes fixed on the shape of the departing riders ahead, Chet jigged his own creature down the road.

So Tom Hudson was prompted to activity because Luke Starn wanted him? The implication was significant.

Chet's trailing did not lead him far. On the outskirts of the town he saw the horse which was ahead suddenly

119

halt outside a house. The two men dismounted.

Chet Wayne jigged his own animal into an alley and quickly found a post to which to tie the reins. He strode swiftly back to the spot where he could get a clear view of the house.

With a shock that was like a douche of iced-water, he realized he was staring at Carl Simister's home.

He knew all the queer tales that circulated about the preacher. The galoot was a ranting hypocrite to most people except, apparently, those who were stupid enough to listen to him.

Sheriff Tom Hudson's words about " — marrying yore sister to thet skunk — " flooded back to Chet.

He strode across the road, hands close to holstered guns. He was through with thinking. His hunches were grim and terrible. He did not know the answers but he figured to find out — pronto!

The door of the house had opened and the two men had gone inside. As Chet came across, the small house

120

seemed deserted, but he wondered what devilish play was going on. Was Jane inside the house?

Chet thought there were ways of finding out.

He was cat-footing around the house, to the back, in a matter of seconds. More, he had one gun drawn.

He found a window that was not shuttered, and the rough, wooden frame was not locked. There was obviously no one in the room beyond. Chet pushed up the window frame with one hand and sidled through the space.

He was in a sparsely-furnished back bedroom. He strode impatiently to the door, but he turned the knob as carefully as possible. He did not want to advertise the fact that he was inside the house.

He guessed the others were in the room which looked out on to the front street. Well, he was going in, too!

Chet stepped into a passage, saw another door in the gloom which was outlined by light beyond it escaping over the edges. He heard the mutter of voices.

He gripped the handle and then thrust open the door and walked right in.

His gun was the most prominent feature to the party inside the room!

"Don't draw unless yuh want a slug!" lipped Chet, and he surveyed the startled occupants.

Luke Starn froze, but his dark eyes glittered as his brain darted over a dozen thoughts. Rory Blain reddened with almost uncontrollable rage, but the gun in Chet's hand checked him.

Sheriff Tom Hudson seemed suddenly haggard, and after the first sharp glance at Chet Wayne he stared bitterly at the floor. Carl Simister swallowed nervously and was the first to speak.

"What — what's the meanin' o' this, Deputy?"

"I figure to return the question to you," drawled Chet. "What goes on here — but don't tell me; I can guess!"

Jane could not control a sort of

gasping sob; it was really reaction.

Chet stared keenly.

"Yuh don't want to marry this galoot, do yuh, Jane?"

"No — I — " The few syllables slipped out.

"Reckon that's enough for me," drawled Chet. "Any other galoot think different?"

There was silence for a moment; and then Luke Starn broke it with a sardonic retort.

"Yuh figure to uphold the law, Deputy, or jest make 'em up as yuh go along?"

"If yuh figurin' to have a wedding right now," said Chet grimly, "I kin tell yuh it's illegal in this State between the hours of 10 p.m. and 8 a.m."

"Yeah?"

"I reckon he's right, Starn," said Tom Hudson quickly.

Jane thrust long fingers over her face as if the strain was too much. Chet said harshly:

"Walk over to me, Jane! Yuh're on

the wrong side when yuh stay over there."

With a sudden movement she darted over to him. She stood behind him, her face pale and wondering.

"Sheriff, I reckon we want this hombre for questionin'," said Chet grimly, and his gun indicated Rory Blain.

"Why?" grated Tom Hudson.

"One o' the jiggers who kidnapped Doc Harper dropped a hat," explained Chet grimly. "An' that hat belongs to Rory Blain. Are we takin' this galoot along for questions, Sheriff?"

"If thet's the way yuh want it," said Tom Hudson heavily.

He was trying desperately to maintain his status. He knew Chet was suspicious of him.

"All right!" snapped Chet. "I figger there ain't goin' to be any weddin', Starn, tonight."

"Yeah?"

"Maybe never," added Chet.

He paused while he eyed the gambler.

124

Luke Starn seemed amused again.

The man knew there was nothing concrete against him as yet. Chet had broken up the wedding simply because the ceremony was illegal during those hours. That was all.

Luke Starn did not realize that Doc Harper had talked to Chet. The young deputy did not want to reveal that. Doc Harper's safety was at stake. And Luke Starn did not know that Chet Wayne had killed Mulaney and knew where Dan Grig was located. Chet kept silent on those points.

But Luke Starn was well aware that Chet must have plenty of suspicions about him by now. Well, being a deputy sheriff was a notoriously dangerous occupation and if something happened to Chet Wayne that would be that. The suspicions would die with him!

"I ain't a-goin' along to the hoosegow," said Rory Blain harshly.

Luke Starn had thought swiftly.

"Why not, Rory?" he said smoothly. "This galoot figgers yuh're bin up to some queer business. Wal, yuh go along an' show him yuh got a clear sheet."

"What the hell d'yuh mean?"

"Jest do as the deputy says," repeated Luke Starn. "Seems we kinda made a mistake. Jane an' me cain't git married tonight but there'll be another time." Luke Starn's dark eyes sought out Jane's and challenged her.

"What if this hombre throws me in the jail?" snapped Rory Blain. "This galoot is tryin' to put a loop on me. If he had thet durned hogleg back in leather, it would be different!"

As if by magic Chet Wayne promptly holstered his Colt. At the incredible speed, even Luke Starn's face hardened.

"The hogleg's back in leather," said Chet grimly. "Maybe yuh want to make somethin' out of it?"

It was a challenge to anyone to draw.

Rory Blain seemed to swell with rage and humiliation. He just glowered, but he made no attempt to go for his guns. Luke Starn kept his hands very much clear of his holsters. Tom Hudson had his arms folded. Carl Simister just looked terrified.

Then the next moment Chet produced two guns and pointed them firmly at Rory Blain. This time two Colts surveyed the group.

"All right," snapped Chet. "I don't figger to stand here all night. Are yuh comin', Rory Blain?"

Luke Starn said quickly:

"Yuh'll be all right. Git goin', Rory. Maybe this jigger is itchin' to plug yuh."

At last the hint penetrated Rory Blain's head. Luke Starn had said he would be all right. Sure, Luke Starn had a hold over Tom Hudson and Tom was the sheriff and not a blamed deputy!

Chet watched closely.

"If yuh want to ask me questions, let's git!" sneered Rory. "Yuh ain't got nothin' on me, Deputy, and yuh never will have."

Chet had a mind as quick as Luke Starn's, and he realized the gambler intended to pull some trick later.

For a moment, Chet wished one of the two men would make a play for hardware. Out of Colt fire there might come a definite settlement of the problems.

But Luke Starn was going to play it the tricky way.

"Wal, if we're goin' back to the office, let's git goin'," said Tom Hudson sourly.

Chet backed to the passage, gun still prominent. The others filed out to the front door.

With Jane standing beside him, Chet watched Luke Starn vault to his saddled horse which was nearby.

"*Adios, segundo!*" called Luke Starn. "Don't worry about the deputy, Rory. He jest wants to play around. Tell him some stories." Then in a harder tone: "I'll see yuh again, Deputy. Maybe yuh won't bust the next play!"

And then Luke Starn wheeled his horse and galloped off into the night.

Chet Wayne compressed his lips.

Although he had succeeded in stopping a terrible marriage, he had a hunch Luke Starn was riding back to the cabin at Snake's Hole.

If Luke Starn figured Dan Grig was a menace . . .

Suppressing this thought, Chet snapped:

"All right, Rory Blain. Yuh're goin' into the hoose-gow while I ride on business. Thet all right, Sheriff?"

They were walking slowly to the centre of the town.

"What charges you got, Chet?" asked Tom Hudson slowly.

"This galoot kidnapped Doc Harper."

Wisely, Chet did not say much more. He knew quite well the setup was a bit of bluff. Tom Hudson could use his authority to set Rory Blain free the moment Chet's back was turned.

Chet Wayne did not hint that he wanted to stack up a murder charge against Rory Blain. And he would — if he could get to Snake's Hole with some reputable citizens who could listen to a deposition from Dan Grig.

"Say, if I've got to spend the night in the hoose-gow — " began Rory Blain angrily.

Chet felt growing irritation. There was so little to hold Rory Blain. He had to get more evidence lined up. Then maybe Doc Harper would speak out in public.

They were walking slowly, with the horses on lead. Chet summed up his thoughts impatiently.

"Tom — yuh can take this galoot back to the office and throw some durned questions at him as to how come he lost his hat when Doc Harper was kidnapped an' hustled out o' his home. Tell this young hellion that such exploits are an offence agin' the law even if the Doc returns apparently unharmed. Jane — if yuh want to ride back home to the Double X, I'll go with yuh. I want to ride out thet way in any case."

He had summed it up. He knew darned fine Tom Hudson was playing along with Luke Starn and would see that Rory Blain was not held to any real purpose.

If Tom Hudson was under Luke Starn's influence, taking him out to Snake's Hole to see Dan Grig would serve no good purpose. If Tom Hudson was helping Luke Starn, he would obstruct any progress to getting a statement from Dan Grig.

"Can yuh do thet, Tom?" asked Chet.

"Whar are yuh ridin'?" asked the sheriff gruffly.

"I told yuh — takin' Miss Jane back to her ranch. I also want to ride around and look for sign o' the robbers that took Dave Guarde's gold."

"Lookin' fer sign at night ain't easy," said Tom Hudson slowly.

"Dave Guarde told yuh about the robbery?"

"Shore. This blamed town's full o' owl-hoots!"

It was all bluff. It was just word-play. Tom Hudson was striving to retain his status.

"Jane — are yuh ridin' back with me?" Chet made his appeal.

She answered slowly, not realizing that the young deputy was burning with impatience.

"I'll ride back home with you, Chet Wayne."

She did not say anything more.

Rory Blain seemed to accept the situation.

"Watch thet galoot, Sis!" he jeered. "He's tryin' to throw a loop over me — jest like he did with Bernard! Remember, he killed Bernard!"

With a muffled gasp, Jane turned to her horse and vaulted to side-saddle. That was her only reply.

Chet was in saddle leather within a second. He leaned forward on the saddle-horn.

"Be seein' yuh, Tom. Maybe yuh can git some explanation out o' that cuss about his hat. You do that, huh?"

"Shore. We can talk." Sheriff Hudson was curt.

Rory Blain and Tom Hudson accepted

the situation. It was a get-out for them, in a way. It would give them the opportunity to talk the situation over.

Chet jigged his horse sideways, making Jane's animal move on. Within a few seconds the two horses were jogging down the street.

There was silence between them for the first few moments, and then Chet broke it.

"I want to pick up another man. We're making a detour around by the Gold Nugget. Then we ride out."

She had not intended to speak, but curiosity got the upper hand.

"Why do you want to pick up another man?"

"I aim to ride around for sign of the robbers."

"I don't know anything about this robbery."

"Wal, some hellions shot up Dave Guarde's Concord," he said briefly. "Men were killed an' the gold was lifted."

"Tonight?"

"Jest a few hours ago — while I was asleep," he said grimly.

Fears shot through her.

"Do you know who robbed the stage?"

"There were four jiggers but the stage guards who could identify them are dead."

"Four men!" she choked. "Do — do — you know them?"

They rode back through an alley and turned into the main street. They were again heading for the shafts of yellow light that flooded from the saloons.

His horse was rubbing flanks with her animal, and he leaned close to her and touched her arm.

"Jane — I want to help yuh! Yuh know that! Don't worry about this robbery."

"You think Rory was mixed in it." She whispered. "No — no — he wouldn't kill! Oh, I know he's hot-headed — but he wouldn't kill!"

He realized he had to clear her mind; tell her the truth.

"Rory was in it," he said heavily. "Luke Starn is bossing a gang. They've got Dave Guarde's gold. One of the outlaws — a hellion name o' Dan Grig — was badly wounded in the affray. I had to kill another rannigan — a feller called Mulaney."

"This — is — awful!" She hammered the words out. She sat up straight in the saddle. "Rory — oh, Rory! What a fool!"

"Rory and Mulaney took Doc Harper out of his home — kidnapped him — an' took him to see this Dan Grig feller so thet the Doc could patch him up. Rory lost his hat in the process. Jane — I'm afraid it's goin' to end bad for Rory. What can anyone do?"

Deep in her heart she realized the truth of his words. But kinship was thick. She tried to defend Rory to the bitter end.

"Luke Starn has a hold on Rory. He owes him money and . . . " Jane paused, realizing that if Luke Starn's story was true Rory had killed a man in Abilene.

She almost choked again. It was useless to tell Chet Wayne about this, for he was a lawman.

"Luke Starn has a grip on others beside Rory," said Chet. "He has somethin' on Tom Hudson. I don't know what it is. But Tom isn't the man he was once."

"Luke Starn sent for him, wanting him as a witness for — for — the . . . " Jane's words tailed off.

"How come thet galoot is throwing a marriage ceremony on you?" asked Chet grimly. "Do yuh want to marry him?"

"No!"

"Then how come?"

"Oh, I can't tell you everythin'!" flashed the girl. "Luke Starn is absolutely ruthless!"

Once again she stumbled at informing Chet Wayne that Rory was responsible for a killing at Abilene.

Chet suddenly dismounted and threw his horse's reins to the girl. They were right opposite the Gold Nugget.

"I'm a-goin' in for a friend. Just stick, Jane. I don't figger to be long."

Chet was as good as his word. In less than three minutes he emerged, and with him were two men.

One was Walt Carr and the other was no other than the old-timer who had found Rory Blain's hat. Ezra Sloan rolled out of the saloon with Chet and Walt Carr as if kind of proud to be in their company.

There was slight delay while Walt Carr got his horse from a nearby livery. The rancher rode a handsome roan, a big horse with plenty of guts.

As he jigged forward, he brought another led horse. The mount was for Ezra Sloan, and was borrowed from the livery.

"Let's git!" said Chet impatiently.

Horses dug hoofs deep in the dust and jigged forward. Soon the party made a rapid tattoo of hoof-beats as they rode out of the town.

Half-way to the Double X spread, Chet Wayne decided that Jane must go home accompanied by Walt Carr. He was uneasy. He did not know where Luke Starn had gone. Maybe the hellion had ridden out to inspect his stolen gold — wherever it was cached — or maybe he was contacting some hired owl-hoots. But on the other hand, if he rode to Snake's Hole and found Mulaney dead and Dan Grig lying helpless . . .

The answer was obvious.

Chet Wayne would have longed to take the girl to the ranch himself, for there were lots of things he had left unsaid, but his duty was plain.

Before he rode off in another direction with Ezra Sloan, he gave Walt Carr instructions in a low voice.

"Meet me at a shack near Snake's Hole. We'll keep this Dan Grig jigger alive till yuh git there. I'd shore like to git that statement, an' I want reliable witnesses."

Walt Carr nodded, jigged his horse to Jane's.

"I'll ride over an' see yuh tomorrow,

Jane," Chet called out. "May I do thet?"

"Yes. I'd like to see you," she said in a voice so soft he barely heard the reply.

And as he jogged off under the moonlight with Ezra Sloan, her simple reply was a great heartener.

"Yuh're new to this town?" Chet asked the old-timer presently.

"Yep. Bin hyar afore though. Reckon Laredo's gittin' mighty lawless."

"It is," agreed Chet. "There's a boom, what with the railroad workers an' gold findings. Some rannigans figger to horn in the dishonest way on thet boom. Yuh know this ride might be kinda dangerous? Not right now, but if a certain hombre gits to know yuh're sidin' with me, you'll be in bad."

Ezra Sloan cackled as if highly amused.

"Young feller, I bin in trouble all me life! Yep. Reckon I got a gift fer gittin' into trouble."

"Right side o' the law?"

"Mister Wayne, I ain't never drawed a gun 'cept in self-defence or to help the weak or the wimmen." Ezra Sloan cackled again. "I was a great feller fer the wimmen when I was younger!"

Chet could not help laughing. The old-timer was something of a tonic. There may be troubles, with Tom Hudson following a grim path and Rory Blain providing unpleasant complications between Jane and himself, but there was some sort of relief in a laugh now and then.

No time was wasted on the ride. Ezra Sloan was double Chet's age, but he had apparently been born in the saddle.

The wan moonlight was a steady but ghostly illumination for the ride. The horses were rowelled into a full lope regardless of holes in the land. They headed across the sage-covered land. The horses avoided the tall clumps of Joshua trees and skeleton-like ocotillo cactus in the full flight across the terrain. As the pace became relentless, there was not the opportunity for words. The two men settled down to grim riding. As they approached the foot-hills, they heard a coyote baying mournfully at the moon. The lone sound rose above the clop-clop of hoofs.

In time the shack near Snake's Hole loomed up out of the jagged territory. At two hundred yards, Chet Wayne reined in his horse and Ezra followed suit.

"Looks kinda quiet," muttered Chet.

He was searching for sign of another horse, but he could not see one.

"Let's git in that shack an' see this galoot!" grunted Ezra Sloan. "I take it this jigger is a bandit an' yuh want a statement from him?"

"Yuh got it right, pardner," returned Chet.

They dismounted. Chet went into the lead, taking his horse along by hand.

Ezra Sloan spat a stream of tobacco juice to the sand and shale.

"Looks like I'm a-headin' fer trouble agin!" he ejaculated.

Chet felt some relief when he

observed no horses near the shack. He had been afraid that Luke Starn might have ridden out to Snake's Hole.

He approached the shack, saw the body of Mulaney lying in the sandy soil.

Ezra Sloan gave the dead man a glance and spat. He hitched up his belt and his one Colt. He looked around at the silent bluff serving as a background to the shack. With moonlight playing on the scene, there was an eerie sensation.

Chet Wayne walked to the shack door. He thrust out a hand to push the pine door open — and then stopped dead!

He had heard a slight sound from inside.

The noise had been little more than a scuffle — a single sound as if someone had moved.

Thoughts flashed through Chet's mind. Dan Grig could hardly be walking around the shack. The man was suffering from serious loss of blood and just had not the strength.

142

Chet did not think Dan Grig was waiting for him — but he had a grim idea that someone else was!

Chet was a lean tense figure at that moment. But be did not pause longer than was necessary.

He kicked at the shack door and then leapt back. As he retreated swiftly, he managed to push Ezra Sloan behind him.

The next instant a gun flashed from the shack! A slug tore through the doorway and sped into the night!

An ejaculation that was not polite escaped Ezra Sloan's lips! A gun appeared in the old-timer's hand as if by magic. The old desert tramp apparently knew how to draw fast on a smokepole!

Chet Wayne hugged the shack wall, tensed for the few moments during which the echoes of the shot died away. There was one grimly-humorous point — Dan Grig had not gotten off his bunk to fire that shot! For one thing, when he had left the outlaw, the man did not possess a gun. And for another, the man was seriously weak.

There was a grimmer thought — possibly Dan Grig was now no longer in the land of the living!

7

"JUMPIN' Jackrabbits! I thought yuh said thet jigger was wounded!" jerked Ezra Sloan.

"He could be dead now!" muttered Chet. He touched the old-timer's arm. "Shuffle around to the end o' this shack an' watch thet window. Yuh wouldn't like a slug in yore hide!"

"I'm mighty tough," cackled Ezra. "I kin make a flap-jack out o' snake's grease and desert dust an' eat it, but I reckon I cain't digest lead!"

"Git movin'!" urged Chet.

The next second the old-timer slithered towards the end of the shack. Boots rasped on loose shale.

A gun roared again and a shot cut through the rotten timber of the shack. The slug whined out into the moonlight.

The vicious shot certainly galvanized

145

Ezra Sloan. He sidled to the end of the shack, turned bright inquiring eyes to Chet.

"Make for that pile of rocks!" urged the deputy. "Now!"

The two men hit the pile of rocks which lay less than fifteen yards away. They slithered into hiding with spurts of dust and rock chips flying from their boots.

"Holy heck, we're now on our bellies like blamed side-winders!" ejaculated Ezra.

"Yuh wouldn't like to be on yore back like a dead coyote, would yuh?" asked Chet, falling in with the other's queer brand of humour.

"Who's in thar?" barked Ezra.

Chet rested his Colt on the ledge of rock, sighted nicely on the shack door. His blue eyes narrowed, losing any vestige of humour. His big body seemed to blend with the rocks. Once, as he moved even closer to the rock, moonlight glinted on his deputy-sheriff badge. There was a tight expression on his face.

"There's a feller in that shack," he said slowly, "who didn't reckon to be caught out like this. That gink is Luke Starn!"

"The hombre who's bossin' a gang?"

"Yep. A galoot who's fixin' up a lot of trouble in Laredo. First he fixes the sheriff an' then he aims to marry a decent gal on account he has her fool brother hog-tied. An' plenty more. Him an' his hellions robbed Dave Guarde, but I reckon two of the outfit won't be able to take much interest in the booty."

"Mebbe we kin make it three?" rapped Ezra, and he poked his Colt over the rock and fired.

Reverberations clanged from the bluff. Gunsmoke drifted past the two men. The shot had sliced into the shack. But there was no retaliation.

"Lyin' low," said Chet thinly. "Wal, I reckon Luke Starn has got to come out o' there with hands high an' start explainin'. If that jigger Dan Grig is dead, I want to know why he died. An' if some galoot put another slug into him to stop him yappin', I guess it'll be too bad for this other galoot!"

"How yuh goin' to git him out?"

"Bein' a lawman, I got to give him the benefit o' the law," retorted Chet.

He raised his voice and shouted. Challenging words rang across the waste.

"Hey, Luke Starn, come on out an' start talkin'. Keep yore hands up."

The echoes died away. And there was no answer — not even a shot!

"Reckon I plugged him wi' thet slug I loosened off?" asked Ezra hopefully.

"I didn't hear a yell," said Chet.

"Why, Mister Wayne, I useter plug badmen right a-tween the eyes. Mebbe I got this jigger thet a-way!"

"Yuh fired blind!" Chet reminded the old-timer ironically.

"Wal, shout agin," urged the other.

Chet bawled across the intervening space.

"Are yuh comin' out, Luke Starn?

We want to parley."

They waited but the same odd silence prevailed. Chet raised his Colt and fired into the ground near the shack.

The clamour died away but no returning fire roared across the wasteland.

"This is damned queer!" Chet gritted.

"Mebbe I kilt him — " began Ezra.

"If he's dead, good riddance," snapped Chet, "but somehow I don't feel thet way!"

He suddenly rose to his feet and raced across the space to the shack. He thudded up to the wall, paused for a split-second check. There was still no shot and still no movement.

He waved Ezra to stay in the rocks. Then he sidled swiftly to the shack door. He looked into the dark, open space. No gun belched flame and lead in his face. There was silence.

There was not even the breathing of a wounded man!

Chet strode in. The oil lamp was not lighted. He knew where to find it — on a rough table at the side of the wall.

He did not understand, but obviously Luke Starn was not in the shack unless, as Ezra claimed, the man was lying in a dark corner . . . dead . . .

Chet thrust fingers into his shirt pocket for a match. He struck the sulphur head on his boot sole and then, as the yellow light flared, stared around.

Dan Grig still lay on the bunk. But he looked very motionless. He was obviously dead.

Then, jerking his head, Chet got everything.

Right in the centre of the room was an up-raised trap-door which was really part of the floor. Chet stared down at a black gaping hole. There was a hole leading down into what was the earth.

A tunnel! The thought struck him right away. And a tunnel always led somewhere!

So Luke Starn had gotten away. That explained the silence after his second shot.

Chet felt sure the man had been Luke Starn. He had ridden out to contact his men — only to find one dead and the other an obvious liability.

But many points were mystifying. Where was Luke Starn now?

Chet strode to the doorway, and almost blundered into old Ezra Sloan, who was approaching with unnecessary cat-foot steps.

The answer to Chet's inward question came at that moment. As if Ezra's approach to the cabin had been a signal, a rider and horse dashed out from the bluff.

The first warning was the thud of hoofs on shale. Then the snort of an animal as rowels were cruelly applied.

Chet wheeled and whipped up guns.

The rider had emerged from the old mine tunnel in the bluff. The pattern of events clinked into place in Chet's mind, but there was not time for more than a split-second thought concerning it.

He triggered into the darkness, with

a grim imprecation as he realized he was seconds too late. The rider was even now a misty shape in the thin light. The horse jerked and sprang to avoid obstacles. With incredible speed, the target was almost nil.

But Chet had flung two shots. They must have cut past the rider and probably spooked the horse into fresh, frantic effort.

Ezra added to the din by throwing a couple of shots into the night. The slugs just tore after the rider and were probably miles wide. In fact, they most likely goaded Luke Starn into rowelling the horse for all it was worth.

Chet turned and raced back to where his horse had been ground hitched. But the shots had spooked the animal, and, together with Ezra's cayuse, the two horses were wheeling aimlessly farther down the run of the bluff.

Time was wasted in getting to the horses and forking them. Chet got to the saddle, urged his mount on. He rode into the night for a few hundred yards, in the direction Luke Starn had taken, and then halted. He compressed his lips with annoyance.

The gambler desperado had used the time to really move. The terrain had swallowed him. The moonlight afforded only a limited amount of visibility, and in fact, the light was deceptive. Chet wheeled the horse again, jigged it up a rocky slope, thinking he might see better at the top.

But there was no positive sign of Luke Starn. He had got away. And tracking him was too slow, because reading sign by night meant a speed of about half-a-mile an hour!

Chet jigged the horse back down the slope to meet up with Ezra Sloan.

"That cuss has gone!" he snapped.

"I don't git how come he done it." roared the oldster.

"I'll show yuh," said Chet thinly, and he led the way back to the cabin.

They stared down at the black hole in the floor of the shack. Chet let the match burn down half-way and then he let it fall into the shaft. Then he struck another match and put it to the wick of the lamp. Soon a steady yellow light illumined the cabin.

"The miners must ha' made this shaft under the shack for some durned reason," said Chet. "Evidently it leads back to the mine tunnel. Shore looks like those miners must ha' had trouble with some jiggers afore the vein ran out."

"I seen this sort o' idee afore," rapped Ezra. "Reckon thar must ha' been some fightin' around hyar one time. Say, thet jigger had his hoss in the mine tunnel!"

"Yep. Handy for him, but he's a galoot who doesn't overlook a trick." Chet walked slowly to Dan Grig. "This man is dead."

"This the gent yuh wanted?"

"Yeah. Figgered he might talk. He still might talk."

"Him?" gasped Ezra. "This feller's dead — yuh jest said, Mister Wayne!"

"But he might be useful all the

154

same," said Chet grimly. "If this jigger has a Colt slug in him he might prove Luke Starn put it there. Because Doc Harper took the earlier slugs out o' this hellion. Right now there shouldn't be any slugs in the ornery galoot!"

Chet gave a quick examination. It was a distasteful task but not the first time he had been forced to handle stiffs. In the end, he thought he located a new wound above the dead man's heart.

"Looks like a .45 slug!" he rapped.

"Yuh aim to ride this stiff into town?"

"Yeah, I guess so. Could be evidence."

"Reckon it'll make a job fer the gravedigger an need a lot on boothill. Ain't thet an expense fer the town?"

"Yuh old buzzard, the community kin stand a bit o' expense!"

Chet looked around for old cloth to bind around the corpse. If the dead man had to be led into town, he figured it was better to get the stiff well-wrapped up so that blood would not run over horse and saddle.

Chet decided on the dirty blankets which had been the desperado's only comfort during his last hours. He was busy working on the unpleasant task when he and Ezra heard the sound of approaching hoofs.

They both tensed and stared towards the open door. Then Chet shouldered past the oldster and stared out. Then he smiled and relaxed.

"Howdy, Walt!" he called out. "Yuh can ride up. But I reckon yuh've had yore ride for nothin'. Dan Grig is dead."

"Plumb dead," added Ezra unnecessarily.

Walt Carr climbed down slowly from his horse.

"How come? Who killed the man?"

"Could be Luke Starn, but your question kinda raises a problem."

"Anythin' yuh can't solve, Chet?"

"Wal, we didn't git a real sight o' the galoot in this cabin," said Chet deliberately. "I figure it was Luke Starn, but if I had to swear on a Bible in a court o' Law, I reckon I'd have to admit I didn't see the cuss."

In swift, clipped phrases he told the rancher how he and Ezra had almost ridden into a drygulch, and how the man had gotten away down the trap covered shaft.

"So we ain't gittin' a statement from Dan Grig!" remarked Walt Carr.

"Nope. All we kin git is proof thet someone shot the feller for the second time-mostly likely with a Colt .45 so as to shut him up for good. I can make a darn good guess who killed the galoot, but thet ain't the proof I'd like."

Within a few minutes they rode out of the derelict site. The dead man lolled across Chet's horse, in front of his saddle. It was a grim load and no pleasure to carry. But he was taking the dead outlaw into town. Among other things, he wanted Tom Hudson to examine the body. He intended to get Doc Harper to go over the dead man and issue a report. All these activities were part of his duty as a lawman.

He just was not a gunslinger who could ride hell-for-leather after men because he hated them and had no more responsibility than that.

"I figger yuh got Miss Jane to the Double X all right, Walt?"

The other smiled.

"Yep. Mighty nice gal. Told her to bolt herself in thet ranch-house an' git herself a gun. She was kinda upset."

"There's only another man at the Double X," said Chet slowly. "An oldish feller name o' Ned Brant. He rides herd on the few longhorns they got."

"He's a right sort o' jigger," assured Walt Carr. "I reckon those Blain brothers shore neglected thet spread. Might ha' made it pay."

"Too durn wild," agreed Chet. "Longhorns didn't suit them. Reckon they wanted a wild life. Wal, as long as Miss Jane has a man she kin trust, I shore feel better."

Walt Carr and Chet Wayne lapsed into silence as they rode steadily towards Laredo. They let the horses pick a natural track through the patches of cholla and the mesquite thickets. The town was slowly but surely approached. Chet was silent mainly because he was bone-tired again and full of thoughts. But not so with Ezra Sloan. The oldster seemed to gain a new lease of life.

"Shore reminds me when I was a young feller," he gabbled. "Yep. I was a bounty hunter once. Figgered to ride down a yeller-bellied skunk name o' Torenze. This catamount was a Mex — wi' eddycation! My, my, thet hombre shore led me a dance! Reckon I rode from Santa Fé to El Paso an' then along the Chisholm Range to Tucson. Yessir, I was a hardy feller in them days. I reckon I c'd sleep in the saddle, fight a wall of Injuns an' jest about track a jigger through three States! Yep, there was a thousand dollars bounty fer this Torenze. Shore I was goin' to hev a real high time wi' thet dinero!"

"What the heck happened, oldster?" grunted Chet.

"Happened! What happened?" repeated

Ezra indignantly. "Why all thet happened!"

"How about this jigger with the bounty on his head?"

"Him? Aw, him! Why, the doggone idjut got drunk in Tucson an' fell offen his hoss and broke his neck. An' me I'd ridden a thousand miles fer nothin'."

"Where were yuh?"

"Me? I was two miles out o' Tucson at the time. Yessir, I was two mile off a thousand dollars. Reckon thet's as far as I ever got to a thousand bits o' silver!"

Ezra Sloan's bragging had one effect, and it might have been intentional; the ride back to town passed fairly quickly! Soon the horses were wending their way down the main street, towards the sheriff's office. Light from the saloons still flooded out, but two were emptying and the others were slowing down from their previous roaring activity. From time to time, men lurched out and climbed to horseback, allowing the animal to take the homeward trail.

Chet felt reaction flooding him. He was really tired again. The few hours' sleep he had snatched had not been sufficient. He was getting back to the terrible weariness with which he had ridden up out of the desert, leading Bernard Blain's horse.

But there were some duties to attend before he grabbed at his rightful dose of sleep. He wanted to report to Sheriff Tom Hudson and show Rory Blain that justice was hard on his heels.

The time was becoming darn late and he thought the sheriff might have lain down. Walt Carr left Chet when the office was sighted. The deputy thanked his rancher friend.

"Think nothin' of it," said Walt Carr. "Any time yuh want help, sign me on as yore unofficial deputy. I reckon this burg needs a new sheriff, anyway."

With that cryptic remark, he rode away in search of an hotel that would give him a room for the night. It was too late for the rancher to ride out to his spread.

Ezra Sloan seemed to figure he was permanently attached to Chet Wayne! When the deputy lugged the corpse into the stone cell at the rear of the office, Ezra followed. The old-timer stared around critically.

"Jest like all the hoose-gows I ever seen — 'cept there ain't anybody in them cells. Usually got some customers!"

"Slack time," said Chet ironically. "Wal, yuh can go, oldster. Yuh got a hotel room?"

"Hell, me?" Ezra was delighted. "I figgered to bed down wi' my hoss in a livery!"

Chet Wayne thrust a hand into a money-pouch in his trousers. He walked forward. Before Ezra realized it, some money was pushed into his hand.

"Don't git independent on me!" growled Chet.

Chet Wayne walked slowly to the cells. He stared. He fumbled for tobacco and brown papers. Quietly, he made his cigarette and then lit it by rasping match on his leather chaps. He blew smoke out — towards the empty cells!

"Seems like Rory Blain didn't stay long," he said bitterly.

He walked out of the office, to the passage. From there he proceeded to Tom Hudson's room. He knocked on the door.

Chet Wayne got a gruff invitation to enter. Tom Hudson knew his knock. Even so, there was a gun in the sheriff's hand as Chet walked into the room. Chet closed the door, turning his back. When he moved around again, Tom Hudson had replaced the Colt on the side-table.

"How did yuh make out?" asked the sheriff. "Yuh sight them outlaws thet took Dave Guarde's gold?"

Chet thrust thumbs into his belt.

"Rory Blain's gone, I see."

"Yep. Couldn't keep him. He hadn't anythin' to say. Findin' his hat don't make a charge." Tom Hudson's voice was harsh.

Chet decided to accept defeat on

that point. Arguments were futile. Suspicion was useless. The only thing that mattered was real down-to-ground proof that would hang a man by means of a trial and jury. He would work until he got just that for Rory Blain and Luke Starn — and any ruffian they might hire.

And in the end Sheriff Tom Hudson would emerge discredited. Chet felt sure the man was protecting Luke Starn.

"I brought back a dead galoot," said Chet clearly. "Got him out in the cell now."

Tom Hudson was lighting a candle. The flickering light threw into relief the haggard lines of his face. The sheriff jerked a glance at his deputy.

"A dead man! What's his name?"

"Dan Grig."

"Huh! Yuh kill him?"

"Nope. He was half-killed by the guards on Dave's Concord. This Dan Grig was one o' the outlaws. But the rifle bullets didn't kill him."

"Yeah?"

"Dan Grig was killed by another galoot who put a Colt slug into him to stop him talkin'."

"Who was this other galoot?"

"I figger it was Luke Starn," said Chet Wayne calmly. "But I cain't prove it yet."

"Luke Starn!" Tom Hudson gulped. "Yuh ain't got the proof?"

"Nope."

"Look, Chet," Sheriff Tom Hudson made a great effort. "I figger yuh could be makin' a mistake. Luke Starn's a gambler, I grant yuh, but thet don't mean he's an out-an'-out crook."

"I reckon he's been at the root of a lot of lawless doings in this town," said Chet deliberately. "An' I don't like the way yuh stick up for him, Tom. I didn't like the idee of seein' yuh willin' to go as a witness to a marriage between Luke Starn an' Miss Jane."

"Didn't the gal want to marry thet jigger?" growled Tom Hudson.

"Yuh ought to know she hates the skunk. But yuh agreed to be a witness.

165

An' yuh knew it was illegal."

Tom Hudson made a savage gesture with his hand.

"Yuh can git, Chet. I'm a-goin' to sleep. I'll talk to yuh come morn."

It was, of course, more or less dismissal. Chet turned reluctantly to the door and then left.

He returned to the office and jail. He looked sombrely at the dead man.

Ezra Sloan circled around and tried to make a cigarette out of the butts he found in the sheriff's ash-tray.

Chet silently handed the old-timer the makings. There was not a word.

In some ways Chet Wayne thought the oldster had many values. For one thing, he was loyal; Chet could bet on that.

Staring at the dead man, Chet felt bitter dismay. He was no nearer to throwing a loop on Luke Starn or corralling Rory Blain. A robbery had been committed and men killed. Gold, which was the result of hard work, had been stolen.

True, two of the outlaws were dead — three if one included the breed who had arrived to knife Chet Wayne. And Bernard Blain had met up with justice — but that event hardly affected the present setup.

Sheriff Tom Hudson was just evading the issues. He did not intend to help his deputy. In fact, he would obstruct. Chet felt discouraged.

No real report could be made without Tom Hudson's signature. Chet considered Doc Harper. If he got a report from the Doc, what would be the position?

The answer came clear. If Doc Harper signed a statement that he had attended Dan Grig at the shack at Snake's Hole, and that he had learned the man was a member of a gang of outlaws comprising Luke Starn and Rory Blain, then the Doc's life would not be worth a plugged Mexican dollar.

Chet groaned. It seemed he was frustrated.

He wheeled savagely.

"I'm a-goin' upstairs to sleep," he

grated to Ezra, "I've had 'bout four hours in the last forty-eight. Hell, a man can only go on so far. Where are yuh goin'?"

Ezra glanced calmly at the big chair behind the sheriff's desk.

"I figger a hardy coot like me c'd sleep pretty nice in thet arm-chair. An' I kin look after the stiff — see he don't walk away!"

"Go to it, oldster," said Chet. He gave a faint grin. "Put back the bolts, amigo, an' douse the light. I'm a-goin' to thet bunk o' mine. Gawd, I shore need thet shut-eye! I reckon everythin' can wait."

As he walked to the passage, Ezra Sloan called after him.

"There'll be another day, podner. An' I got a hunch yuh'll git yore men!"

8

BUT two days passed which were fairly uneventful for Chet Wayne. He saw little sign of Luke Starn or Rory Blain. Tom Hudson kept to the office and resisted all Chet's proposals to do something about locating Dave Guarde's stolen gold.

Chet rode over to the Double X on the first day of the lull in his feud with Luke Starn and Rory Blain. Jane was quiet and evaded any questions connected with her brother. Chet did not pursue the matter, so far as the girl was concerned.

But his keen blue eyes searched the ranch for sign of Rory Blain. And he arrived at the conclusion that the wild rannigan had not been at home for some time.

Chet returned to the Double X on the second day, and found Jane sitting on a corral fence. She seemed very quiet, almost depressed. He received an impression of a slender girl clad in gaberdine shirt and blue levis, with a new Stetson covering her coiled brown hair.

"Seen Rory?" he asked abruptly.

"He hasn't returned home," she said in a low voice.

He was fooling with the brim of his hat. He looked around the ranch-yard with unsmiling eyes. Then he lifted his gaze to the horizon where the broken land led to the hills. There were intervening miles of meadow-land, with some gullies filled with mesquite bush. A few cottonwoods bunched out on the spread, with their white lint showing. In the distance a group of longhorns followed a lead steer. Of Ned Brant, the elderly ranch hand, Chet saw nothing.

"Yuh had anythin' to do with Luke Starn lately?" he asked.

It was an awkward question, and she resented it.

"He hasn't been around here. And I

hope he never shows up!"

"D'yuh know where the galoot is?"

She shook her head; and then said bitterly: "Probably he's ridin' somewhere with Rory."

"I've asked plenty o' questions in town," said Chet quietly, "but I cain't git a lead on Starn. Thet jigger jest seems to have disappeared."

She tightened her small, capable brown hands together.

"There's more trouble a-coming. I know it! Oh, I don't know what to do!"

He put out a hand towards her.

"Look, Jane, when this grief has blown over I figger to come a-calling for yuh. There ain't nothin' yuh can do right now. Don't make it hard on me that I got a job to do."

She stared over the corral. She did not see the white dust and the sunbleached wood. She was searching her mind.

"I don't want to make anythin' hard, Chet," she said. "I guess you've just got to give me time."

"Yuh forgive me — for — for goin' after Bernard?" he muttered.

She put her hands on the corral fence and gripped hard.

"Don't speak about it any more, Chet! Don't bring it up again. That way I guess I'll forget."

"Yuh've got to forget," he said almost roughly.

"I — I — think you're right! I'm sorry for the things I said at first. I — I was all mixed up!"

He put his hat back on his head; slipped the thongs under his chin.

"Jane, I'm glad we're goin' to be friends again. An' I hope anythin' that happens — I mean about Rory — won't spoil our friendship again." He stared anxiously at her. "Jane, there ain't nothin' yuh can do for that brother of yourn! If there was, I'd try to help, but . . . "

She nodded.

"He's a fool!" she choked. "An ornery, bull-headed fool! And I can't do anythin' to help him! And you've

172

got a job to do! Oh, don't think I blame you! I'll never blame you again!"

And as if her emotions were uncontrollable, she slipped from the corral fence and ran towards the ranch-house. Chet Wayne made no attempt to follow. He realized she wanted to be left alone.

He rode out of the spread. As he passed the clump of cottonwoods that gave shelter and shade to the ranch, a jay twittered in the leaves. Chet was riding Blackie now. The big horse, like its rider, had recovered completely from the desert trek.

He halted in the shade of the trees and thought the Double X was a spread that could be made into something good by a man with a capacity for hard work. The Blain brothers had never been that sort. They just wanted the wild life for some queer reason. Jane Blain was merely a girl, and although she was happily different from her reckless brothers there was a limit to the work she could undertake. And the ranch needed money with which to buy new stock and hire good hands.

Looking around, Chet saw the signs of encroaching scrub. There was plenty of work for a hired hand who could get rid of the cholla. Water — he guessed the water-holes would need cleaning out so that the deep springs would continue to flow. A choked spring often diverted somewhere else or lost itself underground. There was decent grass on the spread, stretching right down the valley and up to the broken country where sand and shale took over. He jigged Blackie out of the cottonwoods and started on the five mile trail back to town.

Rider and horse were both big and handsome. Chet Wayne had gotten himself a new green shirt and new black Stetson. Clean leather chaps were tied around checked brown trousers. A yellow bandana was there to keep the dust out of his neck. He looked big, brown and eagle-eyed — a typical man of the vast west. On his green shirt the deputy badge gleamed. At the heels

174

of black riding boots, glinting spurs tinkled as Blackie jogged on.

The big horse never needed spur rowels. A nudge from the rider's knees was enough. More often a few breathed words into the big animal's ears — and the big black horse would stretch into a full lope that would be maintained when other cayuses had tired.

Chet Wayne had covered two miles and the Double X was down on the horizon, a mere smudge if a rider stopped his horse to stare.

The sun was climbing up to its midday position. Chet rode around a thicket of willows. The trail went through Slash B land, and the willows were frequent where water seeped up on to John Wilson's land. Slash B stretched right across the valley, a big spread some fifteen miles long and fronting right into Laredo itself.

Chet saw the two riders approaching him the moment they rode into view. He kept Blackie on at a steady trot and watched the two riders.

He was not a man who surprised easily, and when he realized he was actually riding towards Rory Blain and another unknown hombre he merely smiled thinly. Well, he had been looking for the man!

Even as he rode forward, Chet realized he had nothing final against Rory Blain. He had wanted to keep check on him and maybe quiz him; but as yet he still had to find evidence that would tie the young buckeroo up with the deaths of Dave Guarde's riflemen.

Chet had not yet asked Doc Harper for his statement. The Doc had told him plenty, but that was all unofficial. When there was enough on Rory Blain and Luke Starn to hogtie them, Chet figured to get Doc Harper's written statement and that might clinch the case.

The steady jog of the horses decreased the distance between the men. Chet Wayne did not know the man with Rory Blain. One thing was certain; the galoot was not Luke Starn.

There was no evading the meeting. Chet had no desire to ride off the trail. Grimly, he wondered at the irony of Fate, the joker who handed out this sort of play.

So Rory Blain was riding back to the Double X? Where had the rannigan been the last two days? Out of town, no doubt. Maybe he had been simply lying low. Maybe that had been Tom Hudson's advice. Or maybe the young hombre had been away on some lawless mission with Luke Starn.

The other riders had sighted him, and the horses were slowed to the steady five-miles-an-hour pace which a good cayuse can keep up all day if needed. Soon Chet could make out that Rory Blain's companion was a hard-looking cuss with a moustache.

Chet had not seen the man before, but that did not mean the hombre was new to Laredo. But he did know that a man who rode with Rory Blain was a galoot with no respect for the law.

Birds of a feather — he recalled the old saying.

They met up close by a thicket of pinon and some tallish juniper. The meadow slanted and farther up the slope water trickled from a spring. Not far away cattle moved slowly and lazily, not caring to leave water and green grass.

Chet halted Blackie and leaned forward on the saddle-horn, easing himself from the saddle. Then, slowly, he turned the horse so that it was sideways to the others. They knew what it meant. A man could shoot from the side of his horse better than over its head.

"Howdy, Deputy!" bawled Rory derisively. "Yuh still ridin' alone?"

"I've been to see Jane!" snapped Chet.

"I told yuh to keep away from the Double X," said the other unpleasantly.

"She's worried about yuh," stated Chet. "I figger it's a shame she has to worry about a galoot like you."

Rory Blain's mouth twisted uglily.

"By hell, Wayne, you an' me shore got no love fer each other. Yuh seem to git in my way. Right now yuh got thet hoss astride the trail. I'm askin' yuh to move an' let a hombre pass."

Chet indicated the green grass.

"Plenty o' flat land."

"Yeah? Why should me an' Slim Ward ride offen the trail?"

"I'm particular about the galoots I turn my back on," said Chet drily. "Yuh seen yore boss lately — Luke Starn?"

"Never seen him!" sneered the other.

The glib denial made no pretension at being the truth.

"This yore new podner?" Chet nodded to the man Rory called Slim Ward.

"Jest a feller I know. What the hell's it to yuh?"

"Better tell him Luke Starn has a short way with rannigans who git to be a nuisance — like Dan Grig. Starn killed thet jigger, didn't he? Starn rode over to the cabin at Snake's Hole an'

179

shot the hellion just so as to shut his mouth for good."

"By heck yuh talk a lot, Wayne!" Rory was losing his calmness. His voice thickened. "But yuh all damned lip! Yuh can't prove anythin'. Turn thet hoss. We're ridin' past an' we ain't gittin' offen the trail for any blamed deputy."

The two men jigged horses forward, but Chet Wayne did not turn Blackie.

He knew Rory Blain hated him with deep-seated, slow-burning fury. The galoot would welcome the chance to put a Colt slug into him. But even Rory Blain did not want the shooting to take place on an open trail a few miles from town, where riders might be expected to pass at any moment. Even Rory Blain did not want to be openly branded an outlaw with his name and picture on 'wanted' posters.

Chet guessed the rannigan would prefer to shoot it out under conditions which favoured him. Maybe even a bushwhack bullet. Because Chet's speed with a holstered gun was well known.

Slim Ward rode his horse to the left of Chet. Rory Blain went around on the right.

It was Rory who started the play.

His horse came around the rump of Chet's animal at an angle. Chet sat motionless, watching with eyes that crinkled at the corners.

Then Rory Blain made his play. Swift as a rattler striking, he whipped forward, leaning over from his saddle. His hand shot out and grabbed at Chet's boot.

The grinning young buckeroo heaved on Chet's boot with the speed of a sapling springing back. The deputy was undoubtedly taken by surprise. His boot came out of the stirrup and he began to slide backwards over Blackie's rump.

Chet clawed for the saddle, but missed his grip. Blackie jigged a little, not understanding this strange business, and Chet slipped down to the ground. One foot tangled with the stirrup and he had to shake it loose.

The next second he was aware of two men rushing around on foot to attack him. Chet tried to slither clear, but a boot crashed into his side, almost winding him.

He realized the galoots wanted a rough-house, but with the odds in their favour.

Gritting his teeth, he scrambled away, like a dog. He just had to get clear. He saw Slim Ward lurch after him, his teeth white as he grinned his delight. Chet staggered to his feet, skipped to avoid a vicious kick. Then he drew out a right hook that swept up with ruthless force summoned by his terrible anger.

Slim Ward took it on the lips and the whiteness of his teeth disappeared in a red welter of blood. The blow also stopped his rush. The man staggered back a bit.

Chet Wayne turned as Rory Blain flung two fists low to the stomach. Chet hacked at air as one fist connected. The buckeroo's other fist got blocked by Chet's arm. Then the deputy was almost doubled, gasping for breath. Rory Blain grinned triumphantly and figured he had his man licked. He had beaten up Chet Wayne once before. He thought he would do it again.

He lurched in to plant some more vicious punches. Chet saw the man move, and he evaded the move desperately. He gulped air, felt his nausea subside.

Rory hissed angrily and steadied. He approached Chet with care and yet still maintained some speed.

Slim Ward had returned to the rough-house. He had wiped blood from his mouth. He moved in towards Chet from the side.

Chet Wayne realized grimly that it takes a good man to beat two other tough hombres. But he was damned if he would accept a beating from these jiggers!

Rory Blain was swinging fists and moving in. Slim Ward was poking with an iron-hard right.

Chet gulped more air and dug his

feet into the earth. He dredged up all his strength and courage. Mixed with rightful anger, he slammed into Rory Blain. He was not waiting for the other to pick his blows!

Chet's fists burst through the other's guard and rammed home. A blow rocked Chet. Swiftly, he threw a blow back in retaliation. Then began a slamming match, with two men facing up. Slim Ward tried to butt in and Chet moved his position so that the rannigan got in Rory Blain's way.

Terrible blows hammered home and men gasped. There was the dull thud as fist met hard flesh. There was a hissing sound as men fought for breath. They spat blood and saliva. Boots crunched on loose stones.

Chet fought well and actually recovered from the earlier foul blows. He gave the two men no chance to inflict further low blows or kicks.

More than that, he planted some real hurtful punches into Rory Blain and had the satisfaction of seeing the buckeroo stagger. Chet followed, swinging blows into the galoot. He hurt him. Some of Chet's punches swung up from low down and rammed into Rory Blain with terrific force.

Chet fought like a mountain cat which is cornered. He ripped into Rory Blain when he found the rannigan was tiring. A furious rataplan of punches knocked Rory to his knees. Chet figured the man was not down until he hit the dust, and so he slammed two, three merciless punches into the other's contorting face.

Rory Blain sagged and fell over.

Chet whipped to deal with Slim Ward. That hombre was less confident. He did not advance, and when Chet strode forward a pace, the man backed. But his fists still weaved.

Chet sprang with surprising speed. He closed the gap and plunged punishing fists into the rannigan's face. They connected, rasping down an unshaven jaw. More blood appeared on the galoot's face. He swung furious arms

185

in self-defence. A blow scraped down Chet's face, but he never felt it. He figured to beat this man before Rory Blain picked himself up.

Slim Ward soon uttered choking sounds as Chet battered him ruthlessly. Chet's arms were working with superenergy. Driving him on was a terrible anger which the other two had not reckoned with.

Slim Ward crumpled and lay on the ground, his face only inches from it, his body heaving with his exertions. Chet whipped from him, strode to Rory Blain. He found the man scrambling up.

Chet hit him twice with chopping fists that flashed with the speed of light. Rory Blain slobbered and collapsed again.

"I reckon that pays yuh off for thet beatin' yuh gave me!" choked Chet Wayne. "Yuh gittin' up for more?"

He waited, flicking a wary eye to Slim Ward. The man was stirring and glaring at him. Chet thought the rannigan might be tempted to go for a gun.

But Slim Ward evidently figured he was in no condition for fast gun-play. Or maybe he thought that a hombre who could use his fists so well could use his hands to scoop Colts.

Rory Blain stirred, looked up balefully at the deputy.

"Yuh'll git yores someday, Wayne! By heck, I'll not forget this!"

"Yuh aimed to pitch me off'n my hoss and smash me up — with yore pal!" snapped Chet. "Yuh had the advantage. But yuh ain't so smart, Rory Blain. Git that into yore head, feller. Yuh ain't so smart. My opinion is yuh're headin' for a hangnoose — an' maybe I'll help to put it around yore neck!"

Chet walked slowly and stiffly to his horse. He kept his eyes on the two beaten men. He was not sure of anything. Hate could prompt a man to many low tricks, and shooting another man in the back was one of them.

But Chet Wayne got to his saddle

without seeing any other movement from the two men. He jigged Blackie away, in a crow-hopping movement.

Then with a swift nudge of his knees he sent the big horse flying in a full lope that took him away from his enemies in seconds.

He had picked up his hat before getting to his saddle. But he felt mussed up, and was conscious that blood trickled from a split lip. He hoped he was not due to develop a black eye; his right eye felt sore enough!

All the same, he felt some satisfaction in that he had beaten Rory Blain. That rannigan had got the edge on him the last time they had tussled. He had been dead beat with the desert trek. Well, he had got revenge! More, he had beaten Rory Blain's side-kick into the bargain.

The hot-head would not like that. He would ride back to the Double X and probably rage at Jane. He would try to poison her mind again.

Chet Wayne entered town and made for his room at the top of the sheriff's office.

He hitched Blackie to a tie-rail and was about to go indoors for a wash when Tom Hudson came out of the office accompanied by three other men.

Chet recognized the men as engineers from the railroad workings. They were managerial types and were dressed in store suits of tweed, with the pants tucked into riding boots.

There was a furious argument taking place. Chet heard some sharp words uttered by one of the men, and Tom Hudson's slow, drawling protests.

Then Chet Wayne strode forward, and eyes turned to stare at him.

"Howdy, gents! Somethin' wrong?"

"Plenty is wrong, Deputy. We're asking yore sheriff to get a posse together, but he doesn't seem to realize the urgency."

"Those robbers must be miles away by now!" said Tom Hudson defensively. "Yuh spend time chasin' them an' then ride into town an' expect me to kinda round 'em up out o' a hat or somethin'. I tell yuh there ain't no sense in ridin' out hell-for-leather!"

"You're tryin' my patience, sir!" snapped the man. He turned a lean face to Chet Wayne, gimlet eyes boring into the deputy. "I'm Patrick Leadbetter, District Manager for the Texas and Union Railroad Company. We've been robbed of nearly five thousand dollars!"

"That's a lot of money," said Chet steadily. "When?"

"Just two hours ago. A locomotive and car had just gotten into the camp with the money. We had arranged to pay out today. Before we could get the boxes of money into the safe, we were attacked by a band of armed men. A cashier was killed and the money taken."

"Any of the bandits killed?"

"No, the pesky galoots had the devil's luck."

"Did yuh identify any of the men?

190

Know any of them?"

"They were masked!" snapped Patrick Leadbetter. "But I've gone into this and a lot more with Sheriff Hudson! Are you goin' to get after those owl-hooters?"

"We'll make inquiries!" snapped Sheriff Tom Hudson.

Leadbetter seemed to explode.

"Damn it, sir! I'm goin' to say something you won't like! You seem mighty reluctant to go after those blamed bandits! How come?"

"Yuh jest barge in hyar and ask me to ride out like a blamed fool after a dead trail!" barked Tom Hudson. "Ask my deputy if yuh don't believe me — a dead trail never were any good."

"Two hours ago — " began Leadbetter.

"Nearer three now!" interrupted Tom Hudson. "Them hombres will be Gawd knows where by now."

"That's true, but I don't like yore attitude. Maybe I ought to communicate with the District Judge, at Abilene."

"Judge Tarrant is mighty good in a court," said Tom Hudson sarcastically, "but he never rode after owl-hooters!"

Chet wiped his face and moved closer.

"Look, gentlemen, I'll ride back with yuh to the railroad camp. Maybe Sheriff Hudson will mosey along — unless he's figgering to start inquiries in town."

"I'll ride wi' yuh!" growled Tom Hudson. "I'm sorry if I lost my temper, but you gents rowelled me the wrong way. Yuh bin in a fight, Chet?"

"Yeah. A little bit o' scrappin' with Rory Blain and a side-kick feller name o' Slim Ward."

Tom Hudson gave him a sharp look. "What happened?"

"Nothin' much. They acted plumb like a lot of mangy steers. I gave them a hiding."

"Both o' them!"

"Yeah. I owed Rory Blain somethin' for the beatin' he handed me."

"Are we goin' to ride?" asked Patrick Leadbetter testily. "Mister Deputy, meet my colleagues."

He introduced one of the men — a pale-faced man with a pleasant expression

— as Martin Caudry. The other man was Taylor Watt, a small rotund person who was obviously unfitted for riding after bad men!

Apparently they were managers and under-managers of the railroad company and hence their anxiety to retrieve the stolen wage money.

The three railroad men had horses tied to a hitch-rail in the alley alongside the office. They were certainly impatient, and while Chet Wayne could understand their feelings, he realized the wastage of a few minutes was matterless on a dead trail. So he went inside the office, and made for his room where he sluiced water over his bruises. Then, feeling a bit better, he made his way down to the group and vaulted to his horse.

"All right, let's git goin'."

There was some muttered exclamation from Leadbetter to which Chet smiled thinly.

Chet had not heard the whole account of the robbery, and he had not been present when the rail-road men had first tackled Tom Hudson. He guessed Tom Hudson had adopted the wrong attitude, and, unwisely, revealed his lack of enthusiasm.

To Chet Wayne the sheriff's attitude was grimly significant. Did Tom Hudson think Luke Starn and his hirelings were involved in this new raid? Was that the reason for his hesitation? Did he know anything about the robbery? Maybe he had known it was due to come off!

All this was conjecture, as Chet admitted grimly to himself during the ride out of town. They went down the Lassiter Trail which, after two miles, veered away from the green meadows and looped over to the badlands.

The railroad had been cut through the hills on its route from Abilene. The constructors proposed to lay the steel track across the vast valley south of Laredo and push on to Fort Gulch. At the moment most of the work being done was still in the broken country.

After three more miles the land turned arid. But for those with the eyes to see there was plenty in the dry terrain. There were late flowers hiding under creosote bushes and the clumps of purple sage. Here and there were cacti in blossom, vivid pink and some pale lemon-yellow tinged with green. They rode past clumps of saguaro and ironwood. At times Chet saw wash-willows, catclaw and mesquite. Hawks and falcons swooped through cottonwoods and willows. On the ground he saw tracks of lizards and side-winders. The snakes made a queer S–curved track.

All this was there to the observant eye, and Chet Wayne noticed it because it was part and parcel of his nature. These signs in the semi-arid western lands were as readable as a book.

The party of men rode in silence. Maybe Leadbetter was realizing he might have to say good-bye to his firm's money. Whatever it was, the railroad men rode along in grim silence.

The Lassiter Trail pushed into the broken lands and wound into a canyon. At the other end was the railroad camp. Already Chet could see a plume of smoke which eventually rose from a locomotive.

He wanted to ask questions. He felt pretty grim. He was a lawman and the law was being flouted and he felt he was not doing enough to uphold it. In fact, right now, riding to the railroad camp was, he thought, a waste of time. They were riding in the opposite direction to the robbers, very probably.

The lawless always had the initiative, so far as the current crime was concerned. Now if Laredo had an energetic sheriff instead of a soured man who was in the power of a desperado!

Chet jigged Blackie up to Patrick Leadbetter.

"I've got some questions, sir."

Gimlet eyes swept over him and seemed to approve.

"Fire away, young man."

196

"Wal, I'd like to ask if the pay-money was kept a secret — it's arrival, I mean?"

"The men knew they were goin' to be paid that day!" barked Leadbetter. "Sometimes we get the money up a day beforehand — but not often. We've got worries enough cutting this track without asking for more by keeping big money on hand."

"Then the arrival of the money was well known?"

"Sure."

"About a few hundred galoots must ha' known," said Chet grimly. "Some of the hombres yuh employ wouldn't think twice about liftin' the wage money."

"Granted. We have some rough customers."

"Maybe one or two of them helped the bandits. How many owl-hooters raided you?"

"Seemed like there was five. And they all got away, damn them!"

Chet Wayne thought of Luke Starn. Was it possible this was his work?

But there was not a shred of proof. He could hardly suspect the man with justification, because there were other lawless men in and around Laredo. For all anyone knew, the five bandits might have been ex-employees of the Texas and Union Railroad Company.

"These galoots must ha' worked plumb fast to git that money away without being shot up. Yuh must ha' had a guard."

"Sure, we have a guard, but the idiots were lounging. This is the first raid. No one expected any trouble, I guess. We were taken by surprise. Those cusses worked like fork lightning!"

Some time later the party rode into the camp. Men were at work, but they stopped to stare at the bosses and the two lawmen.

Patrick Leadbetter descended from his horse and threw the reins to a stableman. Then, with Sheriff Hudson and Chet, he stamped over to the office buildings.

"This is where the shooting started!"

he snapped. "You can see the bullet-holes! We've got one dead man."

"Did yuh ride after them?" asked Tom Hudson. "How far did yuh git? Which direction?"

"Sure, we went after them. Naturally they rode into the foothills and it wasn't long before we lost track of them."

"Did yuh secure new bills from yore bank, Mister Leadbetter?" asked Chet.

"Some were new, I should imagine. Damn it, we never got the chance to break the seals on those boxes! But we usually get new bills and old ones mixed."

"I was thinkin' a record will be kept of the bills' serial numbers," said Chet Wayne slowly. "When yuh get that record from yore bank, maybe yuh can let us have a copy. We might catch up with some hombre spendin' yore Company's money!"

"Good idea," said the other harshly. "I'll see that you get a copy of the serial numbers."

Chet Wayne turned a hard lean face to Tom Hudson.

"Ain't nothin' here. Maybe we should ride along the trail these jiggers made into the foothills?"

"Anythin' yuh say," said Sheriff Hudson slowly.

There was nothing definite, but Chet got the same impression that Patrick Leadbetter had got; that Tom Hudson hated the whole business of investigation. It was little wonder that Leadbetter had got annoyed. The man was no fool and could read men.

A few minutes later a party rode out of the camp. Patrick Leadbetter had left his companions at the depot. He rode out with Chet Wayne and the sheriff. His purpose was to show the lawmen the trail left by the fleeing bandits.

They had hardly left the camp when a horseman came riding furiously after them.

Chet turned in his saddle to view the rider. After a few moments a puzzled grin spread over his face.

The man riding so furiously after them was no other than old Ezra Sloan! How had he gotten out here?

A minute or two later the old-timer drew abreast with them.

"Howdy, Mister Wayne! Sufferin' snakes I had a heck o' a time gittin' this hoss saddled! These rail-road fellers don't keep many hosses!"

"What do you want?" Leadbetter snapped. "Who are you? Are you working for the Company?"

"I was," said Ezra calmly. "But I quit two minnits ago. Me — I'm a range-hand! I don't unnerstand railroads. Now when I was a young feller I useter drive a stage an' in them days — "

"Have you stopped us just to yap about yore earlier days?" shouted Leadbetter.

"Goldarn, yuh don't give a galoot time to talk!" snapped Ezra. He turned in his saddle, facing Chet. "I was workin' hyar when those bandits come bustin' in. Reckon I could ha' shot 'em dead iffen I'd had a gun handy.

But I'd hung my belt up. Anyways, I saw 'em."

"Saw who, old-timer?"

"Why, thet jigger, Luke Starn. He was bossin' them owl-hoots!"

"The men were masked. An' yuh don't know Starn," said Chet carefully. "Yuh got to be shore, Ezra."

"I know that hombre," said Ezra Sloan surprisingly. "I knowed his build. I know a man the way he sits his hoss. An' I seen Luke Starn the other day. Yep I seen him plenty!"

"Where? That galoot hasn't been in town to my knowledge. Now, look, old-timer, if yuh're spinnin' a yarn — "

"I saw him," snapped Ezra Sloan. "After that night in yore hoose-gow, when I slept in the chair, I rode out o' town. Wal, seein' yuh don't like long stories, I soon fixed my eyes on a jigger riding west. This feller stopped his hoss in a willow thicket, an' I rode up jest quiet an' steady an' a-mindin' my own business. 'Cause I was bent on goin' thet way an' don't see any reason why

I should turn my hoss."

"All right. Come to the point," demanded Chet.

"Me? Shore, thet's what I'm doin'! As I say I was ridin' alawng to these willows an' this jigger a-sittin' his saddle an' smoking. Then another jigger came ridin' around the blind side o' the thicket an' they started to confab. I jest rode on 'cause thet was the way I figgered to ride, and pretty soon I get a good looksee at these jiggers. Then I knows 'em."

"Wal, who were they?"

"One was this Luke Starn. I know him. An' the other" — Ezra slowly pointed a dirty finger at Tom Hudson — "was the Sheriff of Laredo!"

9

"A DAMNED lie!" grated Tom Hudson.

Ezra bristled. Bright black eyes glinted, and even his whiskers seemed to suggest antagonism.

"I reckon if yuh wasn't the sheriff — " he stuttered.

"Cut it out!" rapped Chet Wayne. He turned a grim face to Tom Hudson. "Is that right? Did yuh see Luke Starn yesterday?"

"This damned old coot is crazy!" snarled the other. "I never left town yesterday. An' look, Wayne, I don't like yore questions. Let's git ridin'."

Leadbetter's sarcastic voice butted in.

"I figure we're just wasting time. I don't know what you're talking about, but I do know this yap doesn't get us anywhere."

"We'll ride," assented Chet. He added

sombrely: "We'll talk later, Tom."

Horses jigged forward. Ezra Sloan placed his animal close to Blackie.

"I don't see why this desert tramp should ride with us!" snapped Sheriff Tom Hudson.

"He won't do any harm," rapped Chet. "An' he might be useful."

The party rode in silence, except for the clop-clop of horse's hoofs. There was plenty of food for thought.

Chet Wayne deliberated over Ezra's story. He did not doubt the truth of it. But so far as he could see there was just Ezra's word against Tom Hudson's, and the latter was still the sheriff. And, in any case, nothing could be proved against Luke Starn.

All the same, Chet wondered what the two men had talked about. If Ezra's story was believed, it was evidence that Tom Hudson was in contact with Luke Starn.

Patrick Leadbetter started his horse off into a gallop, and pretty soon the whole party was going full lope over the broken terrain. The railroad executive seemed grimly exasperated, and Chet could not blame him for feeling that way.

They rode into rock-strewn coulées and edged the horses around jagged outcrops. Leadbetter had gone this way before, in pursuit of the bandits before they had shaken him off.

Then Leadbetter slowed his horse and jigged it around. They were at the bottom of a shale slope.

"This is where those hellions lost us off!" he shouted. "I can't read sign, and over shale I figure it's impossible."

"Shale is bad," admitted Chet Wayne. "But a galoot can sometimes pick up the tracks farther on. Did yuh ride over this slope?"

"Yes. Nothing but shale and rocks, and those bandits have three or four directions to take. You can ride to the shale ridge, but you'll find the land is just a maze of rocky outcrops and gullies."

Chet did not take Leadbetter's word

for it. He urged Blackie up the slope. With a clatter of dislodged shale, rider and horse went to the ridge. Chet Wayne stared over the broken land, and then looked around for sign of fast-moving horses.

He had an expert's knowledge of trailcraft. On the soft ground it was easy to read sign. Even on harder terrain a dislodged stone or broken branch revealed a lot. But finding a trail over loose shale was like trying to find a trail at night — a well-nigh impossible task.

For some time Chet Wayne rode his horse around. He stopped several times to lean forward and stare at the ground. More than once he dismounted and got down on his hands and knees to study some gravelly earth that seemed to suggest the imprint of a horse's hoof. But he could not be sure at any time.

Ezra Sloan spent some time in imitating Chet's example. The oldster knew a lot about picking up sign, but the terrain baffled him. He came over to Chet eventually, on foot. His horse was ground-hitched beside Leadbetter and Tom Hudson, who were silently staying put in their saddles.

"There ain't much hope o' pickin' up sign hyar," yapped Ezra, "Mebbe yuh gits a track — then what? Why, it peters out after a few turns through that rocky land."

"Guess yuh're right," said Chet. "Those jiggers must be any place by now. Few hours time, even the slightest trail they might ha' left will get windswept. Still, we've got to help Leadbetter."

"Best place to look fer outlaws wi' money will be right back in Laredo!" observed Ezra.

He began beating dust out of his ancient range garb. He looked at Chet as if he could regard him as the fountain of knowledge. He even winked at the deputy.

"Yep," he repeated. "Best place is Laredo. Never knew owl-hooters who didn't want to spend dinero soon as they got it!"

Chet Wayne recalled the fight he had had with Rory Blain and Slim Ward. Now if Luke Starn was behind this new exploit, it was a sure thing Rory had been involved — and the ruffianly side-kick with him seemed the hireling type. But they had been riding to the Double X.

Ezra Sloan was probably correct about money burning a hole in the pocket of the average owl-hoot; but Luke Starn was a different sort of man. He would keep the booty under stricter control. In the same way, he had probably disposed of the gold stolen from Dave Guarde's stage.

Chet walked back to Leadbetter, taking Blackie on the ribbons.

He stopped beside Leadbetter and Tom Hudson. He wiped sweat from his face, rubbed dust from his lips.

"There ain't nothin' here."

Leadbetter tilted his hat back, glared down at the deputy.

"By hell, so we have to suffer the loss of five thousand dollars!"

"We might trace the dinero later ... in town ... what do you say, Tom?"

"Could be," grated the sheriff.

"That all you have to say?" Leadbetter wheeled on Tom Hudson. The gimlet eyes were fierce again.

"What else d'yuh want me to say? Iffen yuh ain't satisfied, why don't yuh git some private range investigator on the job? But leave it to us. We'll work on it."

Leadbetter pursed his lips.

"I'll formulate my own plans, thank you. Right now, I'm goin' back to the camp. One last thing, I hope you get some real news for me pretty soon."

And without waiting for the others, the man rode off. He rowelled his bronc and judging by the way he rode he was pretty angry.

"Let's take the trail to Laredo," snapped Chet. "Maybe we can find somethin' there!"

"What do yuh figger to do?" asked Tom Hudson slowly.

"Look out for any jigger spending new bills. And when we git the list of serial numbers from Leadbetter, we can hand copies to the saloon proprietors."

"Most of them galoots are too busy swilling rotgut an' Hermosillo beer," grunted Tom Hudson. "I don't think much o' yore idees."

"Have yuh got any notions o' roundin' up these galoots yoreself?" challenged Chet Wayne.

"This is a lawless town!" snarled the other.

Chet got up to saddle leather and faced the other. For a moment he stared sombrely at the older man.

Then:

"Look, Tom, I'm yore deputy. If there's any way I can help, I wish you'd let me know. I'm talkin' about Luke Starn. That gink is crooked. And yuh know it. But Ezra Sloan here saw yuh talkin' to that hombre the other day. That feller asked yuh to be a witness at a weddin' yuh knew was illegal, an' yuh went along. There's things I don't like, Tom. I cain't pin anything down. But if you'd like to talk . . . maybe I could help . . ."

Sheriff Tom Hudson slowly reddened. Anger suffused over his face.

"Yuh're gittin' yore loop tangled, Chet Wayne. And take a tip — keep yore nose out o' my business. I'll run this sheriff's office the way I want. I'm still the sheriff — in case yuh kinda forgettin'!"

And with that he jabbed spurs to his horse and urged it down the shale. Inside a few seconds he had rounded a big outcrop and was lost to view.

"Wal, kinda touchy!" muttered Chet Wayne.

"Haw, haw, reckon this leaves us on our own!" guffawed Ezra Sloan. "Fust we gits rid o' Leadbetter an' then the blamed sheriff."

"Anythin' more to tell me about seeing Tom Hudson meet up with Luke Starn?"

212

"Nothin' much. Them fellers jest rode out o' the willow thicket soon as they lamped me. Mebbe they figgered I hadn't seen 'em. But I did! Yep! Saw 'em wi' my own eyes."

"Fair enough," muttered Chet. "It all adds up, but yuh can't string men up on such slight points. All right — I'm ridin' back to town. What the blazes do yuh figger on doin' old-timer? Why the heck didn't yuh keep yore job with the railroad company?"

"Told Leadbetter, didn't I?" yelped Ezra. "Don't like railroads! Musta bin a idjut to figger on startin' work in the fust place! I'll ride back to town with yuh."

"All right." Chet sat tall in the saddle and stared around. Ezra found his horse and swung up with agility which was surprising for his age.

Chet Wayne took a last look around at the barren lands. It was a grim, disgruntled scrutiny. The arid terrain seemed to mock back at him.

There was nothing for it but to ride

back to Laredo. Maybe they would catch up with Tom Hudson, talk to him and maintain the strange truce that existed. Leadbetter would be taking a different trail back to the railroad camp.

The two men rode at the steady pace which suited the horses. Hoofs clattered over rock as they rounded big outcrops and then made way over more shale. Occasional thickets of prickly pear cluttered the narrow passages between piles of crumbling red rock. Once a rattler slithered off a hot rock and disappeared with a hiss into a clump of silvery cholla.

The sun saturated everything with heat. The rocks were baking hot and the sand warm as an oven. There was the smell of hot saddle leather about the two horses. Dust rose slowly, idly from clomping hoofs.

And then, after covering about three miles, a sudden menacing sound hissed through the air.

Wwwhhheeee!

The rifle shot sliced past Chet Wayne with less than an inch to spare!

Chet and Ezra flung from horseback simultaneously with a speed that was almost comical. They slithered into cover together.

Then another bullet sang angrily after them. Wwwhhheeee!

Chet had Colts out, resting on the slab of rock behind which he and Ezra had ducked. The old-timer got out his old gun and glared fiercely around.

"Whar's the hellion! Shootin', by Gawd!"

"That's a Winchester," drawled Chet. "An' only one man. Yuh can always tell by lissening to the shots if there's more than one galoot."

The horses were spooked at first, but settled against a high bluff, heads together as if imparting secrets!

Chet Wayne raised his head cautiously and surveyed the ridge of saw-tooth buttes fringing the trail. He figured the rifle-shots had flashed out from the buttes.

Some galoot had waited for them! It had been the nearest thing to a drygulch!

Certain ideas hardened in Chet Wayne's mind. He gave vent to them.

"Some catamount who kinda hates yore guts — or mine," added Ezra.

"Shore. But how the heck would this jigger know we were here?"

"Maybe we was followed."

"That ain't it, old-timer." Chet's tones became brittle. "The men who would want to kill me didn't follow us along to the railroad camp. Nope. This shooter rode along with me all the time."

"Jest what do yuh mean, Mister Wayne?"

"I figger thet hombre with the rifle is Tom Hudson," said Chet grimly. "The sheriff had a Winchester in his saddle-boot."

"Hell, he wouldn't shoot at his own deputy!"

"He could sack me," said Chet with ironic humour. "Tom Hudson is playin' a bad hand."

"Right now, he got a good hand," cracked Ezra. "All we got is hoglegs against that Winchester. Wal I know some Injun tricks. I reckon we kin wriggle out o' this place an' move from rock to rock. Mebbe we kin work around thet feller an' teach him not to throw shells at us."

"All right," assented Chet. "You go that way an' I'll crawl to the left."

Their first move was a sudden dart to a pileup of volcanic rocks less than seven yards away. The rocks were sprinkled in profusion, like gigantic marbles, and stretched over the next few hundred yards of terrain. Chet slithered away to the left, after reaching the heap without attracting rifle fire from their unknown and hidden attacker. He gripped one Colt and kept the other holstered so that he had a free hand to assist in his passage through the rockstrewn land.

Ezra Sloan was soon lost to sight. Chet Wayne went through the rocky pileup like an angry rattler. He knew his objective — a spot beside the saw-tooth buttes.

Once he paused and surveyed the position ahead. He felt a little puzzled. He raised himself, almost inviting a shot.

The concealed Winchester did not bark. In fact, there was no sound or suggestion of movement from ahead.

Chet Wayne scrambled through a cholla-choked gully, and when it thinned out he darted to the nearest boulder. He was pretty close to the base of the jagged butte. Of course, there were a thousand places for a man to hide, but all the same the lack of firing suggested the attacker had moved off.

Chet figured he was near enough for Colt fire. He scooped out the other gun and fired both Colts at the butte. He emptied the chambers, and then sat back grimly while he swiftly refilled the weapons with slugs from his ammunition belt.

The harsh echoes rebounded from the buttes and died away.

The Winchester did not return fire. In fact, there was only brooding silence of the perpetual rocks.

Chet Wayne rose to his feet and walked steadily to the base of the nearest saw-toothed butte. His keen eyes swept every cranny in the ragged wall for sign of a rifle that might poke cautiously and then belch flame and shell.

But the silence was almost serene. He walked on, a thin smile on his lips, his two Colts steady in capable hands.

He gave a wary flick out of the corner of his eye when he sensed a man move on his right. But it was only Ezra Sloan moving in with Chet as if not to be outdone.

Presently, Chet Wayne realized there was no trick to be encountered; in fact, the rifleman had vanished.

In a few more moments he was probing close to the butte face. He walked swiftly. He had given the unknown every chance to kill him.

Ezra Sloan ran up with his waddling

stride, token of many years spent in the saddle. Together they walked along the wall of the butte, looking curiously into every nook and cranny.

Eventually, Chet found the spot where the rifleman had stationed himself. There was a crack in the butte wall which was only horse-width, and it curved right back into the butte like a natural alley. The man had ridden through. The sandy floor was cut with hoof-marks which were as fresh as a morning.

Walking back, Chet Wayne stooped near the entrance to the crack. He picked up a shining shell case.

"Ejected from a Winchester!" he grunted. "Wal, he didn't git us."

"Reckon he didn't try!" supplied Ezra.

"Yep. Yuh're right. He shoo-shayed off pretty quick. Maybe he changed his mind about killin' us."

"Thet doggone sheriff!"

"Might have been some other galoot." Chet shrugged. "I guess it don't matter.

Maybe somebody was jest tryin' to scare us. Shore was a half-hearted play."

They returned to the place where they had last seen the horses. They found the animals nosing for the sparse tufts of grass. In seconds they took up the reins and got to saddle. Hoofs clattered on shale as they rode out.

"Shore like a bit o' gun-play!" yapped Ezra Sloan, turning black, twinkling eyes to the deputy. "Yessir, ever since my Paw gimme bullets to chaw as a youngster, I kinda liked the sound an' smell o' gun-play! Reckon I should ha' bin a Texas Ranger! Mebbe I should ha' bin a State Trooper! Shore is a pity there ain't some more Injun wars cause I reckon I'd be right thar with my Sharps!"

"Ain't it time you were thinkin' of livin' peaceful?" inquired Chet. "How old are you? Why don't yuh get married an' settle down?"

"Me? Git married? I ain't so old as all thet! Durn it, I've had wimmen runnin' after me fer years — an' they ain't a-caught up wi' me yet. Never will! Reckon I'm too smart fer 'em!"

Chet Wayne chuckled inwardly. This oldster was not afraid of many things. In addition, he was not afraid to boast!

They rode into Laredo some time later, and Ezra Sloan hinted that he was mighty hungry. Chet grinned and pointed to a restaurant run by a Chinaman. The midday sun glinted on a huge steak carved in wood and painted red and fixed to the false front of the building. The false front was, a wooden facade giving the impression that the building had an upper floor whereas, in fact, there was just the ground floor.

"I reckon even the Law has to wait until men eat," chuckled the deputy. "We go in there and eat, *segundo*."

"Mighty fine! Ain't yuh goin' to tackle that blamed sheriff about the shootin'? I'd shore like to smell the barrel o' his Winchester. I figger I kin allus tell if a gun's bin fired not so far back."

"I'll let Tom Hudson stew," said Chet quietly. "Maybe he isn't in town. Tom Hudson has a lot to reckon with sooner or later. I reckon he's forked his bronc on to the wrong trail!"

"All the same ter me."

"When are yuh goin' to return thet hoss an' saddle?" asked Chet. "So far as I figure, it belongs to the railroad company."

"They got a livery in town," grunted Ezra. "I'll lead the critter in sometimes."

"What happened to yore own hoss?"

Ezra shook his head sadly.

"I had to sell that animal. Jest the other night. I figgered I needed some dinero. I guess eatin' comes afore ridin' around an' gittin' saddle sores! Only trouble was I guess I spent most o' the money on red-eye thet night in a blamed saloon! So I'm still kinda hungry an' I ain't got no hoss."

"Yuh shore got yore loop tangled!"

They went into the restaurant and had jerky beef and fried potatoes. The place was fairly full. Ranchers sat at tables in booths next to hungry cowpokes. A nestor and his wife and brood of children, out for the day in town, filled another booth. A black-suited gambler had apparently left the cards to take in some nourishment other than liquid. Two smiling Chinese served, moving silently and swiftly on their errands. There was a warm smell of cooking emerging from the back of the place.

Chet and Ezra finished off with apple tart and sauce, and then on to coffee and a quickly-rolled cigarette. Later, Chet paid up and they emerged to the strong sunlight and the horses standing patiently at the tie-rail.

It was at that moment that Luke Starn rode by!

The gambler and desperado sat on a big bay with an almost insolent assurance. Dark eyes immediately flickered to Chet Wayne, noticing the deputy standing close to the tie-rail. Luke Starn was clad in a dark suit of expensive cloth; black, gleaming riding boots into which his pants were tucked, and a fawn Stetson.

With him were two men who had owl-hoot stamped all over them! One was a Mexican and wore leather clothes and steeple-shaped hat. The other was an Indian — a man with a scarred face and plaited hair. He wore the range garb of a white man. But his shirt was faded and dirty — a mixture of both! In his sombrero a feather was stuck.

"Howdy, Deputy!"

Luke Starn reined his horse. He smiled down at Chet.

"You still helling around?" he drawled insolently.

"I git on with my job."

"Yeah? Don't take too much on, Mister Deputy. Overwork ain't healthy."

Chet tired of the mocking voice. He felt his temper rise.

"D'yuh know anythin' about the wage robbery down at the railroad camp?" he flared.

"Bin a robbery?" asked Luke Starn lazily.

"Five thousand dollars in bills. But

they ain't exactly spendable. We're gettin' the numbers of every bill sent through — and the jigger found cashing jest one dollar will have to answer plenty o' questions."

Chet caught the Mexican looking curiously at Luke Starn. It was just a momentary glance.

"Looks like yuh're goin' to be busy when those hellions start spendin' the five thousand," said Luke Starn gravely. "Wal, *adiós amigo*! We got work to do. I'm figurin' on building a new saloon right on thet corner site in mid town. Shore hope yuh ain't got no objection, Deputy. I reckon this town could do with a new saloon."

"These hombres don't look like carpenters to me," said Chet dryly. And he indicated the two border specimens.

"Jest loyal side-kicks," said Luke Starn blandly.

As the three men jigged their horses away down the street, Chet Wayne remembered Rory Blain's companion.

Slim Ward and Rory, along with Luke Starn's hombres, added up to a tidy-sized band of desperadoes. Dan Grig and Mulaney were dead, but that was a mere detail to men who considered life dirt cheap and their own designs highly important.

"Durned bunch o' mangy polecats, if ever I saw 'em!" ejaculated Ezra.

"Owl-hoots!" commented Chet. "Reckon I'll look through the 'wanted' posters back in the office on the chance one of those galoots is a known outlaw. With Tom Hudson squared, those fellers might git the idee they are safe in Laredo."

Ezra looked shrewdly at the other man.

"They ain't safe," he cackled. "Not wi' yuh around!" Then he added: "An' me!"

Chet Wayne wondered if Luke Starn was serious about his intention to build another saloon. Probably the man desired to acquire new property. He had a sound idea that Luke Starn wanted to be a power in the town. The man figured to gain his ends by any method.

Maybe he intended to pay his carpenters and labourers with Dave Guarde's stolen gold! Surely he would not have the audacity to pay them with the railroad's money? There was one thing about gold dust and chips — it was hard to identify.

10

SURE enough, later in the day when Chet Wayne rode through the town alone, he saw men working on the mid-town site. A gang was levelling the ground and already putting in stone foundations. But Chet did not discern the Mexican and Indian among the workmen. So apparently Luke Starn was creating more property in town for himself. Was he putting his ill-gotten gains into legitimate business?

Chet Wayne watched the men at work for a few minutes, noting that Luke Starn was nowhere near the site. He did not bother to ask questions. He smoked a cigarette and decided grimly that Luke Starn was a dangerous man, but he was not going to get away with it!

Watching the men at work, Chet

Wayne realized Luke Starn was a man with ambitions. They were crooked ambitions and therefore dangerous.

The man wanted power in Laredo. Money and property meant power. He had Sheriff Tom Hudson in his grip already. He could hire men and persuade others like Rory Blain that there were great advantages in siding with his plans.

Moodily, Chet Wayne turned away.

He had looked through the 'wanted' bills at the sheriff's office, but there was nothing on the two men Luke Starn had just brought into town.

Chet Wayne was feeling that he was in a bad spot. With Tom Hudson so unco-operative, and actually antagonistic, there was little a deputy could do. He was hog-tied. Even in this latest exploit — the stealing of the railroad money — he had a baffled, frustrated feeling. Until the list of serial numbers came from Patrick Leadbetter, there seemed little he could do.

Naturally, he intended to keep his

eyes wide open. He would be after the slightest clue. But right now he was terribly disgruntled to realize that men like Luke Starn could flout the Law and get away with it.

Chet supposed Rory Blain would be back home at the Double X. The rannigan would be offering hospitality to Slim Ward — and maybe some spring water to cleanse his bruises!

Chet Wayne did not like Jane being out alone on the ranch with a man like Slim Ward around. True, Rory Blain had a certain amount of protective feeling towards his sister, but if he thought he could control some of the men with whom he kept company, he was a fool.

The more Chet thought about the situation, the less he liked it.

He had seen Rory Blain return home with a ruffianly rannigan, and then he had watched Luke Starn ride back into town with two side-kicks of a disreputable type. In this territory a man revealed himself for what he was by the way he dressed and rode his horse. The way a man wore his guns — or the lack of hardware — was another pointer. A proud horse betokened a considerate owner. A vicious, dirty cayuse told the world that the rider was no good.

So the owl-hooters were riding back into town!

Chet Wayne did not like it. The more he thought about it, the more he got the feeling something was brewing.

Moodily, he rode back through the town.

He reviewed the Starn gang again. There was Rory Blain, a no-good young hellion. He was partnering a ruffian called Slim Ward. They would both hate a galoot called Chet Wayne — if only for the hiding they had just received!

Then Luke Starn had apparently gotten himself a new crew in the shape of the Mexican and the Indian. How many more hirelings could the man obtain?

Laredo was unhappily full of hard men who would use their guns for money. Luke Starn could hire almost any of a dozen desperadoes who liked hard riding and hard shooting before honest work.

So apparently the loss of Mulaney and Dan Grig was made good. It was pretty grim to realize there was an unlimited supply of hellions.

The way Chet Wayne saw it, Luke Starn was the man to watch. If that rannigan stopped a bit of lead in the right place, the chances of a cleanup would be greater. The hirelings might ride out of town but fast!

Sick of inactivity, Chet Wayne moved around the town until he located Sheriff Tom Hudson. The man was in a saloon. It was not the respectable Gold Nugget, but a drab building of bare pine boards and little attempt at elementary cleanliness.

Leaving Blackie tied to a rail beside some assorted animals of various appearance, Chet Wayne walked into the saloon. He had been told he would find Tom Hudson inside.

Chet stared at the sheriff. The man leaned heavily against the rough pine counter. He had been drinking a lot.

"I've jest seen Luke Starn and two side-kicks — one a Mex an' the other an Injun," said Chet. "I figger that galoot is behind the railroad robbery."

"Can yuh prove thet?" asked Tom Hudson thickly.

"Nope. I jest think that way."

Tom Hudson gripped his glass and tossed the contents down his throat. He turned sneeringly towards his deputy.

"What the hell sort o' talk is that? Yuh ought to know a man gits a fair trial in this town. An' afore yuh git a man to a trial yuh got to have evidence afore yuh make an arrest. We got Judge Tarrant to think about. I figger yuh got a spite on this galoot, Luke Starn!"

Chet stared again at Tom Hudson.

"Yuh don't usually drink a lot!"

"Cain't a man drink without yuh stickin' yore blamed nose into everythin'?"

"Shore. Go ahead. Drink!" Chet

looked at the other gravely. A sudden prompting made him say: "Me an' old Ezra Sloan were shot at by some jigger up in the broken country. It was just after yuh left us."

Tom Hudson stiffened. He stared with a flushed face straight ahead over the counter. A little to the left a bartender with discoloured teeth stared curiously.

"That's too bad," grunted the sheriff. "Did yuh see the feller?"

"Nope. We tried to circle him, but he moseyed out."

"Stranger, huh?"

"Wal, we didn't see the galoot."

"This is a lawless territory," said Tom Hudson morosely. "I reckon it's gettin' worse. Right now I wish I wasn't the sheriff of this blamed town."

"Yuh could step down," said Chet quietly. "Maybe yuh need a rest."

Tom Hudson jerked around.

"I cain't step down ... I mean ... well ... I reckon I don't want to. It ain't so easy. I bin sheriff hyar a long time. Maybe I'll be in office for a heck o' a time yet. It all depends."

"Depends on what?"

A strange smile lingered on Sheriff Tom Hudson's face.

"Wal, anythin' kin happen in a town where blamed Colt slugs are circulatin'!"

With that queer remark in his ears, Chet Wayne slowly walked out of the insalubrious saloon. He knew he could get no progress from Tom Hudson. The man had secrets and intended to keep them.

But a man could guess at those secrets. Tom Hudson was in a bad fix. He had been a good enough sheriff for a long time, but now he was under some sort of threat.

Chet Wayne rode Blackie down the dusty street. The horse plodded on while Chet rolled a cigarette and lighted it. He stuffed papers and tobacco into his shirt pocket. At that moment Ezra Sloan appeared on the boardwalk. The oldster waved a hand to Chet.

"Howdy, pard."

"Where've yuh been?"

"Jest rollin' around!" cackled Ezra. "I took thet hoss back to the railroad livery in town."

"Yuh got a cayuse to hire?"

"Wal, no . . . not exactly . . . "

"Git up on Blackie. I'll find yuh a new hoss."

"Yuh got a remuda, Mister Wayne?"

"Nope. But I kin git yuh a good nag. I'll pay the hire for yuh. I want yuh to ride out o' town with me. Can yuh do that?"

Ezra Sloan got up behind Chet Wayne with alacrity.

"Yuh want me alawng as yore deppity?"

Chet smiled.

"Wal, I guess yuh can call it that, if yuh like. We're goin' to get yuh a hoss an' then ride down to the Double X."

"Heh! Heh! Yuh gittin' anxious about thet gal yuh told me about!"

Chet smiled wryly and flushed.

"Could be. Might as well ride to the

Double X. It strikes me as kinda queer that Rory Blain an' Luke Starn show up at the same time."

On the way to the livery, Chet Wayne told the old-timer a great deal about Jane Blain and her wild brothers.

"I had to hunt down Bernard Blain. He was laying for me with a gun, but he got killed first."

"Thet was a nasty break, pardner," rapped Ezra. "Wimmen are queer critters an' shootin' up their families don't pacify 'em. Reckon some o' their families ought to be shot, all the same!"

"Yuh old gun-grabber! Maybe yuh gabble too much! Maybe I ought to leave yuh right here in town an' shoo-shay out myself!"

"Yuh cain't do that!" yelped Ezra. "I got my mind all made up. I'm a-comin' with yuh!"

"All right. Button up yore trap about women, hombre!"

Chet Wayne rode along the dusty street, passing some lumbering freight

238

wagons and skirting drawn-up buckboards at the better-class hotels. Finally he arrived at the livery beside the sheriff's office.

Some minutes later Ezra Sloan was fixed up with a dun-coloured bay and cowboy saddle. Chet went into the office, using his pass-key, and got himself a Winchester repeater. He loaded the rifle and put more steel-jacketed bullets in his ammunition belt clips. Then he went out to Blackie and placed the rifle in the saddle-boot, riding with the rig on his left side in the approved manner of the troubleshooter!

They rode out, with the Mexican wrangler at the livery watching them in smiling admiration.

Soon they were covering the dry trail that skirted the meadow-lands just outside the town. They proceeded at a nice lope and then slowed. Two miles at full lope is enough for the best of horses.

"What are yuh worryin' about, pardner?" asked Ezra Sloan, as soon as the horses slowed.

"Nothin' thet I can put my finger on. Jest don't like the setup. Kinda got a feelin' there's somethin' in the air."

"Jest like a herd o' beef afore a sandstorm," said Ezra wisely.

"Yep. Somethin' like that. Guess I'm jest uneasy."

Ezra Sloan rode the dun horse as if he had been master for years. What was more, the horse knew the rider was a trail-wise man.

The well-defined trail took them through gullies and draws where grass grew lush with seeping spring-water. Then a mile or so farther on, the land changed. The signs of arid conditions were to be observed. Cholla lay in clumps and sandy patches appeared.

But the riders were occupied with their thoughts. They hardly realized it when they approached the Double X spread.

Chet Wayne stared at the distant buildings beside the clump of tall cottonwoods. He visualized Jane there, at work on some household tasks or, perhaps, seeing it was late afternoon, she might be resting with only her needlework.

Blackie plodded on steadily. The distant ranch buildings seemed very quiet. He could not see any activity. There was not a horse in the feed corral. That thought suddenly struck him: where were the horses belonging to Slim Ward and Rory Blain?

Of course, the men might have taken the animals out on some job connected with the small herd of longhorns. The beef might be in some distant gully, searching for succulent grass.

Chet Wayne was not sure what he wanted. He realized he was searching for a lead that would take him to some positive activity — preferably against Luke Starn and any of his bunch!

And then, as if wishing made it so, the break came his way.

It was a small factor, but one he did not like. It caused him to halt his horse and stare.

Ezra Sloan followed suit, screwing up his old eyes to stare at some distant scene.

Down by the ranch buildings, a number of men had emerged from the bunkhouse. They trooped out as one, and strode around to the big, ramshackle barn.

Even from the acute distance, Chet Wayne knew the men. He could not make out details but there was the impression of Luke Starn at the head of the outfit. He was sure Rory Blain's head and shoulders stood out against two other rannigans — and they could be the Mexican and Indian whom Luke Starn had acquired. There was a fifth man, somewhat in the rear as if last to leave the bunkhouse.

"Slim Ward! I'll wager!" ejaculated Chet Wayne.

"Heck, my durned eyes ain't what they useter be!" snapped Ezra. "Once I c'd see an eagle blink its peeper! Say, them's the jiggers yuh want to draw a bead on!"

Chet nodded.

"Them's the rannigans! Now what the blazes are they up to?"

"No good, I guess," said Ezra promptly.

"That's an easy answer, old-timer. I don't like the look of those hombres foolin' around Jane's ranch."

"Don't the spread belong to Rory Blain as well?"

"He has his share," said Chet grimly, "but he won't be keepin' it long judgin' by the company he keeps!"

Chet Wayne watched the scene carefully. His mind was full of conjectures; for one thing, he was wondering where the men had put their horses.

The answer to that small point was soon given. It seemed the bunch were making for the barn.

The small, black, toy-like figures moved — and then the barn door was apparently opened. The next moment horses were led out, and there was some scurrying around as men threw saddle-blankets and saddles on the critters.

"Been hidin' their hosses!" said Chet grimly.

"What the heck fer?"

"Yore guess is as good as mine. But these jiggers are the kind who don't like folks to see what's goin' on."

"Ain't nobody up hyar — 'cept us!"

"Yeah. Wal, they kept the hosses under cover in the barn."

"Cain't ride fast on a fully-fed hoss," said Ezra promptly.

"These fellers use the rowel plenty, hombre!"

Chet Wayne jigged his horse forward slowly. He did not suppose the men below had seen them. For one thing the men were too busy to search the horizon.

Chet and Ezra had hardly progressed more than a few hundred yards when the distant scene changed.

The outfit had apparently fixed up the horses quickly. They vaulted to saddle leather and trotted the cayuses out of the ranch yard.

Chet Wayne allowed Blackie to move

at a slow walk while he watched curiously the picture below.

In a matter of minutes the distant bunch in the hollow had ridden out along a western trail. They were either making for the hills or for some rolling country just beyond the western limits of the Double X spread.

As Chet stared sombrely, he saw a figure move slowly to the ranch-house doorway.

It was the figure of a girl in a dress — Chet could discern that much, and, anyway, the mere sight of her told him it was Jane.

She made no attempt to leave the ranch-house. She seemed to be following the party of riders with her eyes.

"All right, *amigo*!" muttered the deputy. "Jig that hoss into a canter. We're ridin' down."

They rode down the slope with a steady canter. All the time the other bunch of riders were going fast along the trail. All at once the outfit rounded a fold in the land and were lost to view.

Chet Wayne and Ezra descended upon the Double X in fine style. The girl saw their approach and stood at the ranch-house door, waiting.

The deputy of Laredo was the first one to rein in his horse before the girl, and he did so in a cloud of hoof dust.

"Howdy, Jane! Say, what is that bunch a-doin' on yore ranch?"

She came down the porch steps slowly, a rather bitter, unsmiling expression on her usually pretty face. She was completely feminine in a floral dress and her long hair soft and billowing.

"You saw them?"

"Yep. What goes on, Jane?"

"They didn't tell me but — but . . . " She almost choked.

"Has Starn bin botherin' you?"

"No, not exactly. He threw out a hint about — about — marriage after — after — they got through some work. Oh, but it's not that! I'm worried sick about Rory! What will be the end of him?"

Chet Wayne thought he knew the answer, but it was too grim for the girl.

"Where are they ridin'?"

"Somewhere west to the rollin' lands."

"Didn't yuh hear their plans, Jane? They must be up to some mischief."

"I didn't hear much. They've been eatin' here. They were mostly full of coarse jokes."

"By heaven, it isn't right yuh should have to tolerate them!" cried Chet.

"Oh, I know, but what can I do? Rory and Luke Starn brought those men here."

"Durned owl-hoots, every one of 'em!" snapped Chet. "An' they've got somethin' on the board. Where the heck can they be headin' west? Go far enough an' they hit the border."

"Mebbe aimin' to hold up 'nother railroad," suggested Ezra Sloan, leaning on his saddle-horn.

"Kinda doubtful. They'd have a long ride. The way they set off, they didn't look like jiggers bent on a long ride."

Jane walked close to Blackie. She

looked up appealingly to Chet Wayne.

"Couldn't you find some way to stop Rory?"

"He's hell-bent!" said Chet. He reached down impulsively, grasped the girl's hand. "Just don't worry about him, Jane."

"But — but — "

"I can't promise anythin'," said Chet harshly. "Yuh know that, Jane. What can I tell yuh?"

She nodded, almost dully. She turned away, walked back to the porch.

"Yuh got old Ned Brant around?" called out Chet.

She turned to answer.

"Yes. He's out — workin' on some sick calves."

"Fine. Keep him around, Jane. An' keep those calves. Some day yuh might see this land work out mighty fine."

With that he fed steel to his mount. Blackie crowhopped at first at the unaccustomed treatment and then sprang into a full lope and raced out of the ranch yard.

Ezra Sloan was slower off the mark, but he lightly rowelled the dun horse and went after Chet Wayne.

The two horsemen galloped out along the western trail. They levelled together and thundered along in the same direction taken by Luke Starn and his outfit.

After some distance disappeared under dust-raising hoofs, the riders slackened the pace.

"We don't want to rush into those galoots," rapped Chet Wayne. "Jest want to trail 'em an' see what the heck they're fixin'."

"Yuh got any plans?"

"Nary a thing. Just want to watch 'em. Maybe we can catch those hellions at some dirty business. Reckon they don't ride for nothin'."

Ezra leaned back in the saddle. He laughed and patted his single Colt.

"He! He! He! I reckon I'll git one o' them jiggers for yuh, Mister Wayne. Yessir, I ain't too old to sight a hogleg!"

The oldster urged his horse on and

gave vent to a cowboy "Yippee!"

"Yuh'll scare the jack-rabbits!" said Chet. "Turn it off, feller!"

Horses trod hard hoofs to the baked trail in a rapid tattoo. The ride went on.

It was some time later, after riding through rolling land, that they sighted the band of men ahead. Chet and Ezra had ridden down a coulée and topped the ridge on the other side. They had paused. Just ahead, moving slowly through jagged, rocky terrain, was the outfit.

"Right. Easy now!" exclaimed Chet. "I don't want those rannigans to suspect we're on their trail!"

From then onwards the two riders moved slowly and carefully, wending a way through land which became increasingly broken and rocky. Shale slopes stretched on both sides of the many defiles they rode into. At the times when they lost sight of the owl-hooters, they worked from the plentiful sign of hoof-prints. It was easy work, simply needing care at every turn of the land or the men ahead would be warned of their presence.

This went on for nearly two hours, and the heat of the day struck at them up in these rocky, arid lands. They had water in canteens, and more than once men and horses stopped to drink.

Chet Wayne was convinced the outfit were off on some exploit. He did not think this ride had any connection with Dave Guarde's stolen gold or the railroad money; Luke Starn certainly would not figure on hiding loot so far out in these badlands.

No. The rannigans were off on some new mission. That was very interesting and, grimly, Chet Wayne figured to be on the spot when the revelations came.

He began to reckon that the outfit were riding for the border. According to his calculation, they were riding parallel with the Texas-Mexico border. Maybe the men might cross the imaginary line. They would pose a neat little problem because his jurisdiction did not extend to Mexico.

Luke Starn could raise the merry devil over the border, and it would be the concern of the Mexican authorities and not the affair of Chet Wayne, a mere deputy from Laredo, Texas!

"Yuh're a kick ahead, pal!" muttered Chet. "Maybe those fellers ain't goin' over the border!"

The tracking went on. The two men got infrequent sights of the other bunch, but that was enough. Sweat trickled down Chet's face and mixed with trail-dust. Ezra Sloan spat out dust from time to time, despite his past boasts that he could make a flap-jack of rattler's grease and desert dust!

And then at last there came a startling end to the trail.

Chet Wayne and Ezra topped another rise and cautiously stared in the direction they expected to see Luke Starn and his bunch.

They saw the men, right enough, and they saw plenty besides.

The outfit were camped in a hollow in the hills. The land was surprisingly grassy, as if water seeped to this hill-bound meadow-land. And milling around on the large area of ground were close on a thousand head of cattle!

11

CHET WAYNE swept the scene with keen eyes. He missed nothing. He was too busy to speak to Ezra. In any case the old-timer could use his own eyes and brains.

The cattle were newly arrived — that much Chet could discern even from the distance of about half a mile. The grass was not beaten down or cropped, although the beef was very busy nosing for grass. That meant the herd had not been in the hollow long.

In addition to these conclusions, Chet saw a number of other men had swollen the party. He thought there was about five more men, but he could not be sure at the distance. Horses were ground hitched and saddles, provisions, rifles were heaped neatly together. A wisp of smoke drifted upwards from a fire proving the men were cooking or, at least, had been cooking.

All this meant that Luke Starn had ridden out for the rendezvous. The other men had been encamped in the hollow waiting for his arrival.

Where had the steers come from?

That, obviously, was the interesting question. Just as interesting was the query — where were the cattle bound? Just exactly what was going on?

Chet Wayne figured he had some of the answers, but he wanted to look into the setup a bit more before he arrived at a firm conclusion.

So with Ezra he set off on a careful downward track towards the camp. There were plenty of rocky passages to afford hiding. Some of the defiles were hardly more than the width of a horse and twisted and turned a great deal.

Eventually, Chet decided they had taken the horses as far as they dared. He came to this conclusion in a small, rock-bound basin where sufficient grass sprouted to keep the animals interested.

He reached for his Winchester, took

it out of the saddle boot. His boots crunched on loose rock chips as he strode over to Ezra.

"Git down off that hoss, feller. We're trailin' those coyotes a bit closer."

"Suits me!" rapped the other.

They moved on foot through the rocky defiles and shale slopes. All the time the land slanted down into the basin. The two men were not in cover all the time. As they approached a bit closer, they had to exercise real care. They moved swiftly and silently from one rocky hideout to another only when they ascertained they could move without being spotted.

In this manner they finally came to a rocky resting place less than two hundred yards from the camp. They could see most things quite clearly.

There was some beef close to the camp and the grouped men. Two hundred yards was a long view of the brands worked on the creatures' flanks, and Chet could not exactly define the marking. This was one point he wanted to check. Where had this beef come from?

He guessed that there was an easy entrance to the basin — probably from the other end. The cattle had entered that way and, no doubt, would have to leave the same way.

Which brought another question: where were the cattle bound? It was easy to hazard guesses, but he wanted to see the brands.

Staring at the grouped men, as they sprawled and talked and smoked, he saw five of them were Mexican vaqueros. They wore steeple-shaped hats and braided trousers. One gay fellow sang a border song about a señorita.

The men, then, were from over the border.

Chet Wayne signalled to Ezra. He wanted the old-timer to move with him.

Chet figured there was a way around the camp, via a scattering of volcanic rocks, to a point which was really close to the herd. A swift, silent worker could get around the camp.

They started out and soon found the task was ticklish. But they moved with care. Only Ezra muttered silent curses! But they moved so quietly even the rattlers hardly knew of their presence! They were bent low as they darted out of one cover to another. All the time they were circling the men.

Apparently the group were taking it easy for the time being. Luke Starn stood talking to a big vaquero who kept his arms crossed in Indian style. Chet got the impression that this man was the leader of the outfit.

But there was time for only a few of these observations. The main task was to work around the camp.

As they progressed the lay of the land changed subtly. It was easier to work around the owl-hoots than Chet had first imagined. The rocks lay in favourable positions when viewed from new angles.

Eventually, Ezra and Chet were well to the right of the camped men. Chet paused when they reached a large chunk of jagged red sandstone, and he gripped Ezra's arm.

"Look at those brands. Ever seen 'em before?"

"Me, I'm a stranger to these parts."

"That's the Twisted V brand. A queer iron. A 'V' with small bulges on each stroke. The man who owns this beef is Pedro Gonzales — a hombre just over the border. Works the biggest spread this part o' Mexico."

Chet Wayne raised his head and cautiously scrutinized the herd again. After a moment he said:

"There's other brands in this lot, too. I reckon that's a Dotted B steer and that's a Double Cloverleaf. Some mavericks, too. Kinda mixed, this herd."

Ezra Sloan had one word for it.

"Rustlin'!"

"Yeah. An' nearly all of it from Mexico. Thing like this will shore make old Pedro Gonzales mighty sore. That old caballero is a handy gent with a couple of six-shooters!"

"Brought these steers over the border," said Ezra. "Me, I reckon this Luke Starn jigger is goin' into the rustlin' business. Me, I reckon — "

"Anywhere for easy money!" interrupted Chet grimly. "Shore, he'll buy those steers for chick-feed an' sell 'em high."

"Who the heck will take stolen beef?" inquired Ezra, squinting a bright eye up to the deputy. "Shore lot o' work blotting them brands. The mavericks will be easy money, anyways."

"I don't know of any rancher in or around Laredo territory who will take those steers," said Chet slowly. "Unless . . . "

"Unless what, podner?"

"Maybe Rory Blain figgers to pack the Double X range out with 'em." Chet's lean face hardened. "There's grass on the Double X right now owin' to their stock gettin' so low. Looks parched, that land, but there's bunch grass an' that's just as good as corn."

Ezra summed it up.

"Wal, what the blazes are we goin' to do?"

Chet gave him a faint grin.

"We're goin' to do plenty!"

Ezra hauled out his gun.

"Not now!" Chet put a hand on his arm. "Later. Now lissen; these jiggers are waitin' until it gets cooler an' then I reckon they start drivin' this beef. Wal, we maybe ain't got time to ride back to Laredo an' get a posse to ride up here to tackle these hellions, so I figger we've got to give 'em some trouble."

"What sort o' trouble?"

"There are ten men out there. We can't draw on ten galoots . . . but maybe we can git the steers to do the work for us." There was a hard, almost unnatural glint in Chet Wayne's blue eyes.

"Steers?"

"Yep. Maybe this is an awful thing to do," said Chet terribly, "but these rannigans are killers. They've laughed at death many a time . . . maybe they figger they can fool old man death all the time. Wal, they cain't! This is what we're goin' to do, old-timer — an' yuh can back out if yuh don't like the idee."

"Hey! I'm yore podner!" snapped Ezra. "Yuh jest tell me what's to be done an' we git on wi' it!"

"Right! Later, when we can work around to the other end of the basin we'll start a stampede. It would be better with hosses, but we can do it on foot with some Colt fire!"

"A stampede!" ejaculated Ezra.

"Yep. We can sweep those galoots to perdition," said Chet harshly. "Once we git those steers hellin' down the basin to that camp, there'll be no stoppin' them. An' there's no way out that end o' the basin, so the herd will mill around. Gawd help any hombre caught in the open!"

"Smash 'em like sticks!" muttered Ezra. He looked straight at Chet. "Yuh want them jiggers daid, don't yuh?"

"Yep!" Chet's mouth was tight as a trap after the word.

"It's thet Luke Starn hombre, ain't it? Yuh kinda hate that rannigan. Thet right?"

"He has to die some time!" rasped Chet. "Some folks will be mighty relieved when he's dead. I've tried to get him on a legal charge. but he's got Tom Hudson like this!" Chet closed his hand like a claw. "An' he's threatenin' Jane Blain . . . wants to marry her . . . the durned rat!"

"There's the gal's brother out there," reminded Ezra.

"He's hell-bent!" said Chet grimly. "Better for Jane he should git killed in a stampede as hang!"

"I reckon yuh're right," muttered Ezra. "An' I'm with yuh. Shore is a hellish way to die, but those hellions brought it on themselves!"

Chet nodded in acceptance of the other.

"All right. Let's move on."

The decision was made. It was a ruthless decision, but they were hard men.

They moved out of hiding and, still cautious, threaded a way through the maze of rocks that lay like a fringe around the meadow-land in the basin. In time they got so far away from the rustlers that they could proceed at a fast stride without much danger of being observed.

Chet held his rifle at easy and wended past a mesquite thicket. He halted, stared at the herd some yards away. He guessed he was near the bottom end of the basin.

The herd was between them and the men. Owing to the lie of the land, he doubted if Luke Starn and his rannigans could see them. And, in any case, the owl-hoots had no suspicions.

"We could get those steers on the move from here," he lipped to Ezra.

"Goin' to start now?"

Chet turned a grim, sweat-streaked face up the meadow. There were taut lines moulding his face. If Jane could have seen him now, she would have been shocked.

"Might as well," he muttered. "We're right behind the main herd . . . we could start that beef runnin' now . . . all we got to do is get it on the prod!"

It seemed that Chet Wayne was sort of reassuring himself of the necessity for this sombre and terrible move.

He handed one of his Colts to Ezra Sloan.

"Start makin' a row with that!" he said grimly.

That gave Ezra two guns to play with and he, himself, had the rifle and a Colt. He tucked the rifle under one arm, his finger curled inside the trigger guard, the weapon deflected to the ground. In his left hand he gripped a Colt.

"Right!" snapped Chet. "Git out among those steers! Git 'em on the prod!"

Ezra Sloan was a hard-bitten old rannigan and he accepted the situation. If men were going to die, that was the way of the frontier.

The two men ran out over the meadow basin, coming up behind the main body of cattle. The next second shots rang out, barking through the silent air.

There was an immediate scamper from the nearest steers. They broke into a frightened lope and headed for the shelter of their companions.

But more shots roared out.

Crack! Crack! Crack!

Crack! Crack! Crack!

The din seemed to flash from all sides. The scampering cattle wheeled, taking more of the herd with them in their fright. Already, with the first shots, the herd was on the prod. As a bulk, it gathered momentum. The fringe of cattle were milling desperately, trying to escape the scaring gunfire. And the bulk of the herd had started to move. The movement was in one direction — towards the other end of the basin.

Chet and Ezra were busy running across the meadow, cutting off tendencies of some steers to veer back down the side of the basin. The men reloaded as they ran, and then flashed off more shots. The herd really got spooked. The rumble of hoofs increased. Chet and Ezra began to race down the basin, now that the herd was pounding away from them.

They really needed horses. Instead they had a stiff task racing after the spooked herd. Never once did they let up with the well-placed gunfire. The herd were pounding the green grass with frantic hoofs. Bawling rose from scores of throats and filled the air.

A few faint shots came from the owl-hoots' camp. The men had jumped to their feet. Some had fired blindly into the rocks at imaginary targets. Others were running futilely, not realizing exactly what was going on. One or two made for the horses, but they were not saddled.

But the ominous sign of the big herd pounding down the basin told the trail-wise men plenty. Hearing the shots that prodded the spooked herd on, clinched their ideas on the subject.

Chet Wayne and Ezra were racing after the herd now. They pumped slugs over the heads of the bucking, bawling animals. The steers pressed on almost blindly, sheer terror of the unknown noises behind them urging them on. The speed of the herd was increasing and, in fact, the cattle were racing now at full stretch.

Ezra Sloan puffed like an old railroad engine. But he hoofed along after the stampeding cattle with a turn of speed that he had never mustered for years. All the time he pumped slugs over the heads of the frightened creatures. He reloaded the Colts as he ran. A number of strange cowboy oaths and threats escaped his lips. In short, in a grim manner, Ezra Sloan was enjoying himself!

Chet Wayne, on the other hand, was in a terrible mood. He ran automatically, his grim eyes noting any attempt on the part of the herd to veer. When that happened he rushed off with guns roaring a threat. The cattle always veered again — this time in the right direction.

The herd was pounding down to the end of the rock-bound basin. The cattle were stretched out all along the width of the land. When they reached the rocks, they would mill in terrific confusion.

Heaven help any men caught in that mass of thundering hoofs and pressing bodies!

Chet Wayne judged his distances well. Of a sudden he raced over to Ezra on his left and grabbed the oldsters' arm. Chet holstered his Colt.

"Let's git over to the side o' the basin! The cattle cain't be stopped now! They'll reach up among the end rocks and then mill around. Maybe they'll turn an' even shootin' won't stop them! We don't want to be out here when they vere back! Let's git!"

With the old-timer, he raced for the rock-strewn side of the natural basin. They reached the fringe where grass disappeared before volcanic rocks. They reloaded the guns and Ezra handed back his Colt. They moved into the warren of the rocky pileup and thrust in the direction of the owl-hoots' camp.

They could still hear the bawling of steers and the pounding of hoofs. Shots cracked sharp above the confused row.

The rustlers were not shooting at Chet and Ezra. Not a slug came their way. It seemed the rannigans were pumping slugs off blindly. So far they had not seen the two men responsible for the stampede.

Chet Wayne realized some men could escape into the rocky pileup that edged the basin. He wanted to be around to get to grips with those men.

On the other hand, some of the owl-hooters might be killed in the onrush of frenzied cattle. That would save a lot of trouble. Maybe Luke Starn would go down that way. Maybe Rory Blain . . .

Chet almost choked on that thought. Grimly, he wondered what possible alternative there was for a young rannigan who had killed like Rory Blain!

But right now Rory Blain might be dead!

The bawling of cattle was at its height, and Chet Wayne guessed they were on the turn. They would be a boiling mass of tossing horns and pounding hoofs!

And in that furious mêlée, men would be striving to gain safety. Cattle and hacking hoofs would be their enemy and not men!

Chet Wayne reached a sloping rock and he raced up to the peak. He stared grimly at the milling herd. He could not see any men. The cattle seemed to be turning in wild confusion.

He figured the men were either dead or scrambling through the rocks. Probably some had gotten away. He wondered who were the lucky men!

He jumped down and joined Ezra Sloan. With a gun well in evidence, he pushed through a cactus-filled cleft in the pileup.

He was tensed to meet up with an enraged owl-hooter who might be expected to shoot on sight. That was just what Chet Wayne hoped for. Any jigger who started shooting was just his meat. That would mean less men to take back to town.

But at every turn of the rocky cleft he peered grimly into undisturbed ground. With Ezra behind him, he prowled on, moving in a general direction towards their hosses.

He suddenly moved into the path of one of the outlaws. The man was a Mexican. He jerked suspiciously, saw the badge on Chet's shirt. The man's gun whipped up and belched flame.

Chet hardly moved his own six-shooter. He just triggered.

The harsh truth was Chet moved a fraction of a moment ahead of the other. Chet Wayne's gun was cracking when the Mexican was whipping at his own hogleg.

The one shot tore into the man, ramming him back against the red rock and deflecting the man's gun.

The Mexican's gun did explode, just

before it slid from the man's grip, but the slug was inevitably wide.

Chet Wayne turned swiftly, stared all around. He did not want some other hombre poking his head over a rock at the sound of shooting and then loosening off a sneak shot.

But Chet saw no other man. He jerked another grim glance at the Mexican. The man sprawled, dead.

So this man had escaped the milling herd! Who else had gotten out of the way of those pounding hoofs?

"Let's git scoutin' around!" Chet snapped the words over to Ezra. "Maybe we'll meet up with another hombre like him!"

"Thet's one dead!" cracked Ezra. "Yuh want to meet a live one!"

"I want to find out about Luke Starn," said Chet sombrely. "Or Rory Blain."

"Hope the beef got them snakeroos!" snapped Ezra.

They pushed past the dead man. They were two grim men and when they turned an edge of rock their first actions were to poke a gun forward and then move after the gun.

Chet Wayne was conscious of the fact that the bawling of cattle had faded. He thought the herd had milled around and was surging back to the centre of the basin. When the scare passed, they would huddle in a solid mass. So it seemed the height of the stampede was over. What was the damage?

Chet and Ezra moved through clefts and slits and eventually reached the spot where they had tethered their horses. The animals were still there, cropping at grass.

"Yuh stick with the hosses," said Chet quickly. "I'm a-goin' to looksee for those galoots. But I don't want any o' 'em findin' our hosses an' figurin' to make a getaway on them. So yuh stick, pardner."

"Doggone it, I could use a Colt on them jiggers!" rapped Ezra. "I don't aim tuh be a hoss wrangler!"

"You can stop any rannigan who

makes a play for these hosses!" retorted Chet. "I figure those owl-hoots' hosses stampeded with the cows, an' I reckon those fellers won't be likin' to dive back among that herd."

"Maybe thar ain't any o' those jiggers left alive!"

"Maybe. That's what I'd like to find out."

And with that Chet Wayne walked back into the rocky pileup and was lost to Ezra's view.

What the deputy wanted most of all was knowledge of Luke Starn and Rory Blain. What had been their fate? Had they escaped the stampede?

By searching the area, he hoped to get a bead on the men. He could examine the remains of the owl-hooters' camp. If he found any dead men . . . well . . . he could count . . .

Chet reached the edge of the basin without seeing any other man. He paused, sank behind a jutting outcrop and squinted around at the one-time camp.

The fire and the saddles were scattered. Three figures lay prone on the ground but widely separated.

Chet turned his head slowly, warily. He thought he was alone in the scattered rocks. He rose and walked across the churned ground. He went on towards the first prone figure.

The herd was a good way off now and settling again. Chet saw two horses cropping grass near the herd. But there was no sign of a living man.

He reached the first figure and knew the man to be dead before he got really close. There was a terrible patch of blood ... Chet gritted back a desire to vomit.

He stared at the man. He did not have to turn the body. The rannigan would never see another cantina again.

Yeah, the man was another Mexican.

Chet walked on, covering the ground with his fast strides. He reached another figure, stared down grimly.

The corpse was a horrible sight, but he recognized this man as the Indian

Luke Starn had hired.

Grimly, Chet Wayne raised his eyes to stare at the third body.

Was it possible that the next dead man was Luke Starn or even Rory Blain?

Or maybe those two had the devil's own luck.

Chet strode over, determined to reach some conclusions. He came to the third gory body and stared down. He had no trouble at identifying the man as one of the Mexican vaqueros.

He turned swiftly, stared around. So far as he could see only three men had fallen to the hoofs of the stampeding herd. Apparently Luke Starn and Rory had escaped.

Gritting his teeth, he thought luck was always with those who least deserved it.

Chet walked back steadily to the rocky fringe of the basin.

At that moment a gun cracked the air. The slug fell near his feet — a spent force.

The man who had triggered had no patience. He should have waited until Chet was really inside range for a six-gun.

Chet Wayne cradled his rifle and fired back at the spot from where he fancied the Colt slug had emerged.

At the same time, he darted across the land, making for the nearest recesses in the rocks.

So he had been seen examining the dead men. The owl-hoots would know now who had started the stampede.

Chet was grimly sorry that Luke Starn had not fallen under the cattle's hoofs. That would have been one way out.

Chet Wayne reached a haven and ducked into it as another Colt slug bit the dust after him. A rataplan of shots chipped red rock all around him. He lay low, grinning thinly. He could read the play easily. The way the slugs came over proved the gunman was merely satisfying his fury.

But Chet located the trigger-happy

character. As the volley ceased, Chet darted out of his hiding-place and, moving at a crouch, snaked down the bed of a jagged cleft barely man-wide and three feet high.

He was going after the gunman!

CHET WAYNE did not find the gun-fighter. The deputy moved swiftly but carefully through the many clefts, making over to the spot where he thought the gunman might be, but, as he warily rounded each edge of rock, there was no sign of a man.

He did not get impatient. That was the quick way to boothill, he figured. He probed farther through the rocky volcanic pileup. In the end he thought that the outlaws had pulled out. Quickly, he thought over the setup. Maybe the remaining men had lost their guns. Certainly they had no horses in the rocky alleys. The animals had stampeded with the spooked herd. He thought he detected some horses at the far end of the basin. Even so, these cayuses were not saddled and the leather was pounded and flung in all directions.

In a sense he had made some discoveries. It seemed that Luke Starn and Rory Blain had escaped the stampede, along with some other galoots. He did not know what they were doing right now. The rannigans seemed darned quiet.

In the end Chet's movements brought him back to the spot where Ezra Sloan tended the two horses.

The oldster was well alert and had his gun out and pointed at the first sign of Chet's hat!

"Hell! Yuh nearly made me trigger!"

"Seen anybody yet?" queried Chet.

"Nary a sign. Shore heerd yuh shootin' podner! Who was the jigger? Did yuh git him?"

"Yuh're a bloodthirsty old catamount! Nope, I didn't git the feller. I think the rannigans have pulled out."

"Had enough, huh?"

Chet shook his head slowly. He fumbled in his shirt pocket for the 'makings'.

"Don't rightly know whether they've

had enough. I figger they're tryin' to round up again. They need hosses badly. An' they've got to find the saddle leather for them. I've looked for those jiggers but they seem to have vanished. This pileup could hide an Injun tribe."

Ezra Sloan squinted his bright black eyes. Chet finished rolling the cigarette and handed it to the old-timer. Then he started on another.

"What's the play now, Deppity?"

"I figger we should take these hosses back to some place real safe an' then trail back and try get the edge on Luke Starn and Rory Blain."

"Seems right enough," grunted Ezra. They lighted the cigarettes and enjoyed the first few lungfuls of smoke from the black tobacco. Then they walked out of the rock-bound nook, leading the horses by the reins.

Eventually, they came on to sloping land which was mostly shale covered with clumps of cholla. But outcrops of rock thrust abruptly out of the land and assumed towering, grotesque shapes. They decided to hide the horses in a U-shaped nook made by one of these outcrops.

Chet and Ezra rode the animals into the cover and dismounted. They threw the reins over the horses' heads. Some sparse grass, now golden brown, would keep the horses occupied and they would not stray as long as they were ground hitched.

The two horses were quiet on the sandy bed of the nook when suddenly Chet and Ezra heard the fast clop-clop of horses' hoofs!

"Riders!" Chet cradled the rifle. He strode to the edge of the hideout, slowed carefully.

"Two hosses a-ridin' fast!" decided Ezra and he ambled across to a handy spot where he could look out.

They were just in time to see two riders thundering their mounts down a shale slope with sheer reckless speed. The glimpse was only momentary and then a rounded knob of sandy hill hid the two riders.

But Chet Wayne had recognized them, swiftly, certainly.

"Luke Starn an' Rory Blain!" he snapped. "Let's git after 'em."

"Those fellers are shore ridin' hell-for-leather!" cackled Ezra. "Now what the heck's rowelling them galoots?"

But he got no answer. Chet Wayne had whipped the reins back over Blackie's head and vaulted to the saddle. Another second and he had the horse springing forward.

"Doggone it!" cursed Ezra. "Thet galoot is allus ahead o' me! An' him only thirty years younger then me!"

But the oldster was in his saddle as quick as possible and jigging his horse after Blackie.

The deputy from Laredo raced his animal down the slope to the spot where he had last seen the two fast-moving horsemen.

But the other two men had a good headstart, and there was nothing for Chet Wayne to see when he rounded the sandy hill.

He tore on around the base of the hillock. Blackie rammed a tattoo of hoofs to soft soil and seemed to enjoy the gallop.

The terrain was very rough and almost every yard could hide a man and horse. But Chet Wayne figured he would catch up if he rode Blackie hard enough.

The big animal responded. The gap between Ezra Sloan and Chet Wayne widened! Blackie went full lope over some dangerous ground.

Ezra Sloan let loose some full-blooded range oaths.

"Git goin', hoss!" he exclaimed, and added some other expletives. "Yuh goin' to let thet yunker loose me off!"

Chet Wayne thundered along a sandy defile and then slashed around a bluff overhung with silvery cholla and grey sagebrush.

But it was surprising how much headstart the other two men had achieved. They were well in the distance, but it was only a momentary view. Luke Starn and Rory Blain rowelled the broncs down a dangerous slope to a trail below. Chet lost sight at the start.

Apparently all the owl-hoot horses had not stampeded to the other end of the basin. At any rate two had been rounded up, and Luke Starn and Rory Blain had ridden out.

The furious way they were riding seemed to suggest they were getting out. But Chet Wayne did not expect Luke Starn to back out of any tussle so promptly. No, the man must have sound reasons behind the ride out.

When the shale slope was reached, Blackie went down with slithering hoofs. A small avalanche was started. Chet allowed the horse to make its own progress. They reached the trail below with Blackie almost on haunches.

Ezra Sloan took the dun horse down, but from the start the cayuse did not like the exploit. The animal's ears went back and teeth showed in fright. Half-way down the steep slope, with dislodged stones making a clatter, the horse jerked in fright. The animal plunged wildly along the side of the slope. All at once, with the sudden movement, Ezra was thrown from the saddle.

Chet had paused just a few yards along the trail. He had known it was a hard slope to negotiate, but had not expected to see Ezra thrown!

The old-timer rolled over and over until he hit the hard, yellow trail at the bottom of the slope. He lay still for a few seconds.

Chet jigged Blackie around and urged the horse back.

He had hardly gotten to Ezra Sloan when the oldster got up with a roar of rage which Chet heard distinctly.

"Doggone thet hoss! Fust time I ever had a hoss throw me! Fust time, I tell yuh!"

Chet laughed grimly.

"Try gittin' that durned hoss, oldster!"

The dun was now on the trail, standing still with pricked back ears, getting over the fright.

Ezra Sloan scrambled after it, his bow legs moving like pistons. The horse jibbed a bit as Ezra grabbed at the reins, but the old-timer quietened the creature.

Chet wheeled his horse, got the animal back to a full lope. He thundered along to the end of the trail, where the sun-baked land rounded a bluff.

He realized the delay had been to Luke Starn's advantage.

He was right. When he rounded the bluff, the other two men were not in sight.

He slowed Blackie to a canter, and stared at the trail. He could make out the horse hoof-prints. He knew he could follow the trail of the other two men. But he doubted if he would catch up with them. They had got their headstart.

A few moments later, Ezra Sloan rode up. Chet made a gesture with his hand. Together they pounded on ahead, in the half chance that they might spot the two other rannigans.

But it was not to be. Luke Starn and his hot-headed side-kick had benefited by the delay. They were completely out of sight in the jagged country. Chet went on another half-mile, reading the sign, but he knew this pace was miles slower than that of the two owl-hooters.

"Wall, those hombres got away," he grunted at last. He halted his horse, leaned on the fork of the saddle horn. "They were in a heck o' a hurry. Didn't seem disposed to stay an' argue."

"Wal, they left the beef," supplied Ezra. "They cain't leave thet herd in thet basin too lawng. Ain't enough grass in another day."

Chet turned his head, stared back to the strewn rocks which fringed the top of the shale slope.

"I reckon there are some other galoots still moseyin' around up there. Maybe some o' them vaqueros — still lookin' for their hosses. An' I don't know what happened to Slim Ward."

"Yuh figger to go back thar?"

"Yeah. Why not?"

"Ain't no reason I kin figger." Ezra twisted his face and his whiskers bristled fiercely. "I reckon I'd like to git the edge on some o' they buzzards. Me, I don't like fallin' off a hoss, an' I got to take it out o' some jiggers!"

They turned the horses and rode back. They avoided the worst part of the shale slope and reached the top by an easier route. Then they headed back to the V-shaped nook.

Chet had figured it was a good idea to round up some rannigan and get him to talk. Maybe Slim Ward would be the galoot to aim for.

The fact that Luke Starn and Rory Blain had ridden away was not so important as getting evidence against them lined up.

And if only one of the owl-hoot band could be induced to talk, a real step forward would be made.

The horses were broken to ground hitching and would not stray from the nook as long as the reins trailed. Ezra and Chet tramped out and, in single file, edged into the rocky pileup again.

Chet Wayne was first, and his rifle cradled nicely. He knew he would shoot if a man came gunning, but he really wanted the galoot who would open his mouth and talk.

He was not sure what to expect. For all he knew the hellions might have rounded up the remaining horses and ridden out. Of course, the dead men would never ride again; but there were the others unaccounted for.

He knew one thing: if the rannigans rode out, they would return. The herd would not be left to eventually stray out of the basin.

No: they would return. The rannigans would ride in again and try to move the herd.

Chet knew when that would happen — at night!

That was the best time for owl-hoot rustlers to operate. They would be busy at night — maybe that night!

With these thoughts in mind, he

moved through a rocky defile at cautious speed. He could hear Ezra grunting right behind him. They made some noise as they stamped down prickly cactus.

In this way they reached the edge of the grassy basin. They had not encountered another man. Then, looking out over the natural meadow, Chet Wayne observed riders moving at the far end.

They were attempting to work stray steers back to the main herd. Chet counted three men. They had apparently got headstalls and saddles on three horses and got them to work.

Chet made some calculations. Three men out of ten left seven unaccounted for. Two had ridden out to some unknown destination. That left five.

Chet Wayne knew he had killed one hombre and he had counted three dead as a result of the stampede. That still left another man.

Well, maybe the man could not get a horse or saddle. On the other hand, the man might be dead lying in a cleft or some other hideout.

In any case, there were three men out there and the capture of one would be a good notion. He might be made to talk!

Chet outlined his ideas to Ezra.

"We've got to work closer to those galoots an' then get a bead on them. As this herd is rustled, I got every right to take one o' these rannigans in."

"I reckon we kin git the whole three o' 'em!" said Ezra.

"Maybe. Who knows?"

With the few clipped words, Chet Wayne moved on. He was a tall, lean, dusty figure against a background of reddish rock. He rustled past an overhanging clump of grey sagebrush. He turned a sharp edge of the outcrop, poking his Winchester forward warily before completing the turn.

Old-timer Ezra came up behind him, an admiring, satisfied expression on his face. For Ezra was kind of enjoying events! The old fellow had been a wanderer and a hard case all his life, and he wanted to die with his boots on!

Working around the basin was a slow business, but this was the second time they had moved into the amazing scattering of man-high rocks and they were familiar with several clefts or natural alleys. Progress was surprisingly steady and in time they were stationed behind a large boulder barely thirty yards from the nearest owl-hoot!

The man sat hunched on his saddled horse, watching his two side-kicks round up three stubborn steers that persisted in wandering towards the winding, rock-bound entry — or exit — to the meadow. The man had his back to Chet Wayne and his partner. The man seemed to be taking it easy. He was smoking and watching the other two men.

Chet knew the man was one of the vaqueros from over the border who had met up with Luke Starn. The man was one of the band who had brought the rustled beef to this hilly, rock-bound meadow.

The rounding-up was seemingly almost completed. Chet Wayne was waiting shrewdly. He thought one man could get the drop on three. And as Ezra had a Colt which he was itching to use, the odds were fairly even.

The way it happened was simple, and yet the deputy had half expected it. He had thought the man smoking was waiting for the other two.

The other two rannigans rode up to their companion at a canter and halted.

A few seconds were spent in rolling cigarettes. The three riders hunched together to light up.

Chet Wayne strode out, long legged strides thrusting him quickly to the bunch. The Winchester stuck out like a cannon. Chet knew the first few seconds were his; and then he bawled:

"All right! Reach!"

Two men twisted in their saddles. The other promptly shot his hands up above his shoulders. The two who jerked around followed as soon as their startled eyes saw Chet Wayne advancing with the firm rifle. And behind Chet, not to be outdone, was Ezra Sloan. The oldster's Colt was rock steady in his grimy, ancient hand!

Chet felt disappointed that Slim Ward was not among the bunch. He wondered where the man had got to.

The three men were vaqueros. Swarthy faces and glinting black eyes turned to Chet and Ezra. The men sat their saddles easily, hands up past their shoulders. Chet Wayne noted the brands on the horses. He had not seen them before, and he figured they were undoubtedly Mexican.

"Git down off them hosses!" he snapped.

As the situation was entirely Chet Wayne's, there was no alternative for the rannigans but obedience. They slowly vaulted from saddle leather, stood on the ground and did not move.

There was no doubt they knew

that Chet and Ezra were the men responsible for the stampede and the deaths of their companions. But other men dying probably did not worry these hellions. Right now they were most likely figuring out how the present setup would end.

"Move over here," ordered Chet. "Away from them cayuses. Ezra — git around them an' take their hardware."

With a loud cackle of delight, Ezra Sloan ambled around the owl-hooters. He sure approached cautiously around the backs of the men. Then, when close enough, he stuck his Colt into the ribs of a man, at the same time scooping the man's hardware. Ezra flung the guns about five yards and soon had a heap of six-shooters.

Then he ambled around to Chet and stood warily a few yards from the bunch.

"What now, Deppity?"

"First a few questions," returned Chet. "Then these Rustlers go back to Laredo. We got a hoose-gow an' it ain't been used much lately."

He paused, then pointed the Winchester at the nearest Mexican.

"Luke Starn an' Rory Blain figured to buy this beef. An' it's rustled beef. That right?"

The man twisted his lips in a silent sneer. He seemed to be grinning.

"Yuh understand my lingo?" snapped Chet.

The vaquero sneered: "Yeah. We understan'. But we don't say anything, *amigo*. You can go to hell!"

An enraged roar came from Ezra.

"Gawd! I ain't a-standin' fer thet!"

Chet smiled.

"Take it easy, podner. These galoots will talk later. Nothin' we can now do up here. Git up on one o' them hosses, Ezra. I'll take one an' we'll prod these hombres along until we git back to our own cayuses."

That was the way they made the sullen men move. One thought it would be smart to play stubborn. He stopped walking. Ezra promptly leaned down from the horse and gave the man a hurtful clopping blow with the butt end of his Colt. The man stumbled along after that.

Getting through the rocky pileup was not so easy, but was negotiated with Ezra Sloan riding in front of the three men with Chet taking up the rear. Chet had to prod the men on twice with the long-reaching rifle. Unless the hombres wanted to invite a bullet, there was little they could do. Escape was impossible because a slug would reach them faster than they could run.

The third horse followed behind Chet Wayne without a lead rope. They needed three horses because the owl-hoots were due to ride back to Laredo as soon as Chet and Ezra got to their own horses.

Eventually the U-shaped nook was reached and Chet vaulted down and walked to Blackie. He leaped to his saddle, shoved the Winchester into the scabbard and drew his two hoglegs. They looked mighty big guns to the three Mexicans.

"Git up on yore hosses. An' don't try to play it smart. The first feller to make a break gits a slug. Yuh're ridin' back to Laredo an' the hoose-gow on a charge o' rustlin'!"

One of the men spoke up.

"But we are Mexicans! You can't hold us in an American jail!"

"Yeah? I reckon I can. Maybe some Mex sheriff will be interested to hear about the rustlin' an' the jiggers who done it."

And that was the way it was. The vaqueros got to their horses unwillingly, with many dark looks and exchanged glances. But they were without guns, and they knew that to make a dash for it, now that they were mounted, was to invite sudden death.

The party rode away three sullen men in steeple-shaped hats followed closely by two riders who held guns as if they grew in fists!

As they got along the trail, Chet had questions.

"Where is this hombre Slim Ward?"

One of the men turned a swarthy, insolent face.

"We go back an' look, huh?"

Chet shot him a hard glance.

"Maybe, maybe not. Where is the galoot?"

"I do not know, señor. Perhaps we ride back an' look?"

"Nope. I reckon yuh'll ride into Laredo," said Chet grimly. "I'd like to fill those empty cells in the hoose-gow. Maybe yuh know why Luke Starn an' Rory Blain rode out hell-for-leather?"

The man did not bother to reply, but spat dust and saliva contemptuously in the deputy's direction and then turned his head.

The ride went on in blazing heat. Froth fringed the headstalls of the horses and showed at the edges of the saddle-blankets. Men, too, acquired a mask of trail dust which mingled with rivulets of sweat. Chet and Ezra each held a gun, holding the reins with the other hand. They did not intend to holster the hardware. That might tempt

301

one of the rannigans to make a break. There would be only one answer to a breakaway and that would be a slug. But Chet did not want to drive dead men into Laredo. He wanted these hellions in the jail for questioning when they cooled.

They came down from the hills and rode across the plains of the great valley. Over in the distance, behind shimmering heat hazes, lay the Double X spread.

But Chet Wayne was all for pushing on to town. There was to be no side-tracking until these three hellions were off his hands.

He did wonder where Luke Starn and Rory Blain might have hitched their horses. Could it be they had returned to Laredo? For what purpose?

There was no answer to these problems even when the weary ride was over and the buildings of Laredo came into view, with the yellow trail winding into the town.

They rode straight to the sheriff's

office. A crowd collected. Chet and Ezra held guns on the three men as they slowly dismounted.

"All right! Move into the office!" snapped Chet.

The door was open and the passage was bare and inviting. The three owl-hooters walked slowly up the boardwalk, boots rasping. There were crude laughs from the crowd, and one man snarled some angry exclamation.

Chet knew the folks would move on when the little show was over. In a town like Laredo, satisfying a curiosity was legitimate entertainment.

The three Mexicans stomped into the building. Chet moved past them and opened a door. This led to the office and the cells.

Sheriff Tom Hudson rose slowly to his feet as Chet prodded the three rannigans inside the office. Tom Hudson looked morose and untidy. He had taken off his heavy gun-belts. He did not smile; in fact, his eyes held a glint of irritation.

"Who the hell's these jiggers?"

"Rustlers!" said Chet Wayne coolly. "I'm takin' them in until we git some things settled."

"What things?" Tom Hudson reached for his gun-belt and slowly buckled it on while his eyes flickered over the men. "There ain't been any rustlin' round these parts for a long time."

"Wal, it's kinda long story," said Chet. "I figger we want a lot o' things settled. Maybe these ginks will talk. Right now I want 'em behind the bars. A feller cain't relax with these hellions around!"

That job required some gun-prodding and manhandling at the last minute because the Mexicans jibbed at the sight of the barred cells. But finally the three men were locked in separate cells, and the big bunch of iron keys returned to the nail above Tom Hudson's desk.

"Wal, I'm waitin' to hear aboot these jiggers," grunted Tom Hudson. "Where the hell did yuh round them up?"

Ezra Sloan drifted out to satisfy his

thirst. Chet told Tom Hudson about the finding of the rustled herd high in the hills, and the trailing of Luke Starn and Rory Blain to the rendezvous with the vaqueros. He did not hold anything back in his accusations against Luke Starn or Rory Blain.

All the time he spoke, he knew Sheriff Tom Hudson was seeking for holes in the setup.

"What 'n hell would Luke Starn want with rustled beef?" rapped Tom Hudson.

"If he worked with Rory Blain, that beef could be run on Double X land. Plenty o' gullies an' draws to hide a lot o' stock on that spread. I tell yuh, this beef has mostly Mexican brands. Those hellions in them cells could tell us jest how the herd was driven to that meadow basin."

"What do yuh aim to do?" asked Tom Hudson slowly.

"Hold these fellers until they cool. Then git some depositions. In the meantime maybe I can cut sign o'

Luke Starn or his side-kick. They might be in town. Then I reckon some cowpunchers ought to be sent up to git that herd down out o' that basin. Those critters might stray when that grass gits thin. An' I'm mighty interested to know what happened to a jigger called Slim Ward."

"Yuh got it all figgered out," said Tom Hudson slowly.

"Yeah. But I reckon I'd like it all tied up," said Chet coolly.

"There's a job for a deputy down at Santos Wells," said Tom Hudson harshly. "Some jigger down there reckons his neighbour poisoned a well."

"Swear in another deputy," said Chet grimly. "I got plenty to do without ridin' down to Santos Wells. That's more than a day's ridin'."

With that he went out of the office.

13

CHET strode out into the street. He paused to use his bandana to wipe sweat and dust from his face. Then he tied the kerchief around his neck again. He thought he would ride out to a desert water-hole if he ever got a chance later and have a swim around in cool water.

He paused when Ezra Sloan waddled along the boardwalk to meet him.

"Yuh finished tellin' thet sheriff the whole spiel?"

Chet unhitched the reins holding Blackie. He turned his attention to Ezra's dun horse.

"Yeah, I told him."

"Think he'll help any?"

"Nope. Soon as Luke Starn knows we got those three hombres jailed, he'll be after Tom Hudson to let 'em out."

"Ain't yuh goin' to watch fer thet?"

"No danger for some time, I figger. By sundown I'll get statements from those jiggers — or I reckon they'll never talk."

Chet handed the ribbons to Ezra.

"Lead these hosses into the livery, podner. They won't be ridin' the trail today. I reckon they've done enough. An' that goes for those nags belongin' to the Mexicans."

The five horses were led into the livery at the back of the office. The wrangler took over and promised to have two fresh horses if Chet and Ezra returned, wanting them.

"Seen anythin' o' Luke Starn when yuh were out wettin' yore gullet?" asked Chet.

"No sign an' no talk," said Ezra. "Anyways, I was too busy drinkin' Hermosillo beer."

"Yuh got any dinero left?"

"Nope. Say, I'm poorer than a blamed nester!"

"Wal, don't worry, *segundo*. I figger I need some beer after that ride down from the badlands. You come with me!"

There was no need to persuade Ezra Sloan. He gave an exclamation of joy and ambled after Chet Wayne. They made a curious pair as they walked down the main stem. Chet Wayne was tall, hard-muscled, straight-backed. Ezra was bent and bow-legged with much riding.

They consumed two ales in a nearby saloon and had a look at the assortment of characters who were in drinking and playing faro that late afternoon.

The characters took little notice of the badge-toter and less notice of Ezra Sloan. Some of the men drinking red-eye were not exactly exemplary individuals; Chet knew some were loungers who worked only when other methods of obtaining money failed. A few were range-hardened cowboys who had gotten some time off. Others were labourers apparently enjoying a separation from their tasks.

"Anybody seen Luke Starn ride into

town?" asked Chet.

The question rang through the bar hut brought no response. Some men turned to stare at the deputy, and others shook their heads and resumed drinking or talking.

"Must be a ghost rider!" grunted Chet. "Nobody ever sees that hombre at any time!"

They strolled out of the saloon on that. Chet stood with Ezra on the boardwalk. They rolled cigarettes, lit them and paused in thoughtful silence.

"We got to make some arrangements fer gettin' that herd down from that basin," said Chet, at last. "If we git that beef down in Laredo stockyards, it amounts to solid evidence against those hellions I got in the jail. With those brands those jiggers don't stand a chance o' talkin' out of the fix they're in. Then maybe they'll talk fast about Luke Starn."

"Shore hope yuh allow me to ride herd," yapped Ezra. "Reckon I used ter be a top hand wi' ornery steers.

Yuh git the hands, an I'll take 'em up to thet hill basin, Mister Deputy!"

"I was thinkin' of something like that," grinned Chet. "Wal, we got to git the hands!"

They strode through the town. They made for the Laredo Stockman, a saloon much frequented by ranchers and wandering punchers, beef buyers and examiners.

It was Chet Wayne's idea to round up a posse or trail gang who could be hired for the purpose of bringing down the herd. One thing was sure, the cattle could not be left in the hills. For one thing, the herd itself was evidence of rustling. Then it was a sure thing that Luke Starn would not be content to abandon the beef. He would make another throw.

So far the man's venture into rustling had wavered badly. If Luke Starn had thought the acquisition of stolen beef was only a matter of a few days' easy work, he had been disappointed. The task had gone wrong, and Chet Wayne

311

had started the trouble.

They were tramping down a side street, on the way to the Laredo Stockman, when Tom Hudson suddenly appeared across their path. The sheriff halted. He had a Mexican cigar in his mouth and was worrying it pretty badly.

"Thought I caught sight o' yuh crossin' the street," he muttered. "I cut around this-away. Say, Chet, I want yuh to take a looksee at an ornary character who has booked a room at the Bonanza Hotel."

Chet frowned, puzzled.

"Who is this galoot? Look, Tom, I got a lot to do — "

"I hold the office of sheriff around hyar!" said the other harshly. "I'm only askin' yuh to help me identify this feller. This rannigan has jest blown in. I hear he's an outlaw, a wanted man. I don't see why this town should be a hideout fer every blamed owlhoot on the run."

Chet instinctively hitched his gun-belt to a more comfortable setting.

"All right. Let's git. Ezra ... yuh blow over to the Stockman ... I'll join yuh later."

"This old coot can come with yuh," snapped Tom Hudson.

Ezra bristled.

"I ain't so old! An' I ain't a blamed fool, Mister Sheriff! Now lemme tell yuh — "

"Aw, can it, oldster," growled Chet. "Maybe yuh had better mosey with me so I kin keep my peepers on yuh."

"Shore, shore! Anythin' yuh say. Maybe yuh'll need a gun-hand when yuh lamp this badman, anyways!"

Chet smiled.

"Maybe. All right, Tom, let's git!" They strode off, Chet and Tom Hudson taking the long deliberate strides of men more accustomed to the saddle than tramping. Ezra Sloan ambled along with them, bright eyes gleaming his satisfaction at his new importance.

"Those jiggers in the jail still all right, Tom?" asked Chet slowly.

"Yeah. Still under lock and key, if thet's what yuh mean."

"Thet's what I do mean, Tom. They'll cool. Maybe we kin git some answers out o' them tonight."

"It ain't no easy chore being sheriff of this blamed town," grumbled Tom Hudson. "A man can't tackle everythin'. Some o' the folks don't want law."

"What sort o' people don't want law?" asked Chet.

Tom Hudson tightened his lips. He did not answer, and then they turned a corner and were beside the Bonanza Hotel.

It was a dirty place in contradiction to its name. The false front was covered with peeling paint; the porch had several worn, loose planks. Two loungers, leaning against the clapboard walls, were unpleasant looking specimens.

Chet knew the place as a cheap sleeping-place and saloon. The property had been up since the early days of the town's growth, and the ownership had changed hands frequently.

Tom Hudson gave the place not a second glance, but led the way on to the creaking porch boards. He pushed through the swinging bat-wing doors, and then stood to one side as Chet and Ezra entered.

"This galoot is upstairs," said Tom Hudson grimly.

"How d'yuh know?"

"I got the tip from the clerk."

"Jest who is this jigger yuh're wanting?"

"Hap Verity . . . but he ain't usin' thet name hyar."

Chet nodded his understanding. Hap Verity was a well-known outlaw and there was not a town in the county that would have tolerated him.

Chet shot a glance at the winding flight of stairs. At the bottom was an open doorway which led to the bar-room. To the right of the stairs was a desk with a dirty bottle of ink and a ledger. There was no clerk or anyone else around. Business seemed quiet.

"Wal, are we going up?" grunted Tom Hudson.

Chet looked at him curiously. A red spot was glowing on the other's leathery cheeks. His hands were tight around the leather of his twin six-guns.

A grim thought stirred Chet Wayne's mind. Some of his wary instincts prodded him. He just could not place what was in his mind. Maybe it was just an instinct for danger. But, then, there was bound to be danger in tackling a gunny like Hap Verity.

Chet Wayne did not know why he had a prickly feeling in his scalp. He could not analyse his hunches at that moment.

"Yeah, let's go up," assented Chet grimly.

He did wonder why Tom Hudson had decided to make a set against this particular outlaw. There were other badmen in Laredo who deserved to be run out, and Tom had done nothing about them.

They climbed the stairs slowly, and

as they moved up Chet drew a gun from his holster. Tom Hudson still kept his hands curled around the leather of his holsters as if he just wanted to feel the weight of the hoglegs. Ezra came up last and had not drawn his solitary gun.

In this way they reached a landing which contained no window and was unusually dark. They went along slowly, as men who were taking time to look over every aspect of the situation. Tom Hudson pointed to a door in the passage.

"That's his room. I bin told he holed up there all this day!"

Chet moved closer to the door. He paused.

"Let's rope the galoot out."

Tom Hudson licked his lips as if they were unbearably dry.

"This kinda job ain't so good," he muttered. "I haven't done this kinda work for a lawng time."

Chet raised a fist and knocked on the pine door.

"That'll start somethin'!" he said grimly.

Ezra Sloan drew his Colt.

"Maybe I'll git me a real bad hombre!" he cackled.

But there was no answer to Chet's knocking. The deputy put a hand to the door-knob. He turned it sharply and felt the door open.

"This ain't locked!"

The next moment Chet kicked the door inwards. Gun in hand, he paused.

No Colt fire roared from the room; there was no movement or suggestion of a man lurking there.

"You shore yuh got the right information, Tom?" rapped Chet.

He edged along the opened door. He got past the door frame. He stared at a bed at the other side of the room.

There was a man lying on the bed as if unconscious — or dead.

Chet Wayne felt scalp tingles. He crinkled his eyes narrowly, wondering just exactly what was the play.

He edged farther into the room

— then took three swift steps over to the bed.

He grabbed at the dirty bedspread which covered almost all the man's face. He drew the cloth down sharply.

Chet Wayne did not get the chance to see the prone man's features. With shattering suddenness, something hard struck the back of his head, crashing him to oblivion in a second. He plunged immediately into a mile deep black pit.

Ezra Sloan, who had shuffled into the room some steps behind Chet, had seen the play.

He had seen the closet door at the back of the deputy swing open noiselessly and the gun butt hack wickedly at Chet Wayne's head as he leaned over the man on the bed.

Ezra was powerless. Even as his hoarse yell sounded, Chet Wayne pitched forward.

Ezra whipped up his gun — and the next instant, even as the barrel was swinging, Tom Hudson rammed a thudding blow at the oldster's arm.

The blow was like a mule-kick and agony shot through the old-timer. His arm slammed down. The Colt did not explode, and in the next second it fell from Ezra's numbed grasp and thudded dully on the floor.

The man on the bed jumped up. He flung Chet Wayne to one side, dived over to Ezra Sloan and hacked a wicked fist to the oldster's jaw.

"Take that, yuh interferin' old catamount!" snarled Rory Blain.

Luke Starn pushed his gun back into the holster hidden under his black coat. He smiled triumphantly.

"Wal, you played a real good part, Tom! Yes sir, a mighty good part! Now we've got these skunks jest the way we want 'em."

"Yuh forced me to this," said Tom Hudson harshly.

"Shore, shore. Yuh workin' for me. It's good to have a sheriff working on one's side."

"Don't overplay yore hand, Starn," said Tom Hudson thickly. "Yuh're not killin' these two men."

"No?"

"Nope. I'm the sheriff of this town an' yuh want me as a cover-up man. All right. But kill Chet Wayne — an' this old galoot — an' I'll fix yuh for a hangnoose party."

"That's a threat, Tom," said Luke Starn smoothly.

"I mean it. I'm not having the deaths of these two men on my conscience."

"A conscience is a luxury," sneered the other. "Yuh're not in a position to afford luxuries, Tom. But don't git all hot up. We just aim to keep these galoots out o' the way until we git that herd down from the hills."

Rory Blain stared down at Chet Wayne with hatred in his eyes.

"This damned feller aimed to kill us in thet stampede!"

"Yeah, shore did." Luke Starn's black eyes glittered. His hand went back to his holster, seemed to smooth the butt of his gun. "Yeah, he busted up our play an' killed those rannigans workin' for me. Then he has the gall to ride those Mexicans into town. He gits in my way all times. First he sticks his blamed nose into Dave Guarde's missing gold an' then he figgers he ought to account for the railroad money!"

"Yuh c'd blast him now!" said Rory Blain violently.

"The sheriff says 'no'!" sneered Luke Starn.

"A hombre like him is a danger all the time he's alive."

"Yeah. Shore. But take it easy. Git some rope an' gags on these jiggers. We'll think out ways an' means o' dealing with Chet Wayne. Right now we've stopped him gittin' a crew up to that herd."

Rory Blain moved reluctantly.

"Ain't the way I'd do it. But yuh're the boss."

"Keep that in mind!" sneered Luke Starn, and his eyes swung to Tom Hudson again. "I'm the boss. I know how to handle these jobs. I got ways of doin' things. Take this durned hotel. I

322

own the blamed place an' the galoot who manages for me knows that what I say goes. So he cleared the place for me. Jest in case we had trouble with these waddies."

"Yuh move fast when you want, I grant yuh that," said Tom Hudson grimly.

"Yeah. Wal, yuh got another job. See thet those Mex rannigans are set free. Tell them to ride out o' town. I don't want 'em drinkin' in town an' talking their blamed heads off. They git, pronto! Tell 'em to git back to the herd. We're a-goin' up there to git that herd on the move afore sundown. Rory, here, has got land an' water for those steers!"

Tom Hudson nodded, moved towards the door.

"All right, but yuh play this the way I said. Yuh ain't killin' Chet Wayne — unless yuh git the drop on him in a fair gun-fight. An' that ain't somethin' I kin stop. But yuh ain't killin' these men in cold blood or — "

"Or yuh talk," supplied Luke Starn calmly. "Shore, shore, Tom. But if yuh aim to talk, yuh'll be makin' yoreself a candidate for a hangnoose party at the same time. Yuh aimed to make yourself some easy dinero, some time back, when we stole the Bar 2 Bar hosses. Yuh worked it nicely for me, Tom. Yuh got the Bar 2 Bar crew out of the way on a false posse, an' me and my bunch cleaned the durned hoss ranch jest about out. Yuh got yore cut on the sale o' them hosses. Good money, too. Yuh gave me a receipt, Tom. Yep, and' I got a galoot in this town who can swear yuh to the gallows as a hoss thief, Tom. This galoot is my witness."

"Yuh'd go to the hangnoose yoreself!" said Tom Hudson furiously.

"Maybeso. I reckon we jest say we're all in this together, huh?"

Rory Blain looked up from Ezra Sloan.

"Say, we'd best cut the cackle afore these hombres come round and start yellin'."

"Shore, shore. Now mosey along, Tom, an' play this the way I want it an' yuh'll be all right. Yuh'll be more than that. Yuh'll be my right-hand man with plenty o' dinero an' sheriff o' this town for as long as yuh want. Now vamoose."

"I'm a-goin'," said the other sombrely. "But one last word to yuh, Luke Starn: yuh ain't killin' these two men in cold blood."

"Shore! Who says we want trouble? We'll jest hold 'em safe an' sound until we git thet herd where we want 'em. All right — we want some riders. That's why we rode back to town. We want a trail crew for that herd. Git these two galoots roped and gagged, Rory. We got work to do."

14

SHERIFF TOM HUDSON left the Bonanza Hotel and walked down the dusty street with bowed shoulders.

His grim mind was lashed with self-reproach. He was a hard man, but not devoid of conscience. He was between the devil and the deep sea. He knew Luke Starn could not be trusted, and yet he was forcing himself to believe the man would keep faith.

Tom Hudson was revolted at the thought that Rory Blain or Luke Starne — or for that matter any ruffian hired to press a trigger — might kill Chet Wayne and his old side-kick in cold blood. Yet it was possible. He tried to shut the possibility from his thoughts, but the vision jagged at him time and again.

Tom Hudson almost lurched into a

nearby saloon. He ordered a rye jerkily. He carried the glass over the room and stared through a window. He could see the entrance to the Bonanza Hotel, although at an angle.

It was not long before Luke Starn and Rory Blain walked out of the place and, with the wary glances of men accustomed to trouble, moved down an alley between the hotel and a nearby tannery.

Tom Hudson drank off his rye and stood thinking.

He realized that Chet Wayne and old Ezra Sloan were probably now lying, bound and gagged, in the locked room, with orders to Herman Wein, the hotel manager, to leave well alone and keep folks away from the upper floor of the hotel.

Sheriff Tom Hudson felt like a sick man. He began to think all around the jam he was in. He knew someday there would be a showdown.

He breathed heavily. From his own viewpoint, the only way out would bring death and disgrace.

He walked slowly from the saloon, without attracting attention from the few men outside. He went slowly along the boardwalk, boots rasping on dust-covered pine.

He had known for a long time that he could ride out of Laredo some time at dead of night and never return. He could assume another identity in another town a long way off from Laredo. He could even run across the border. He could take the long trail to far Montana and be lost to those in Laredo. That was one way out. Or he could stick in Laredo and play along with Luke Starn and his lawless plans.

There was another way out. Colt fire could settle many things, and Luke Starn could die as fast as any other man with slugs tearing into him!

Tom Hudson strode on slowly, hardly realizing he was approaching his office. His soured thoughts were confused, and he realized he was unable to find any solution.

Seeing the office building jerked him to reality. He remembered he had to set the Mexicans free and pass on Luke Starn's orders.

He was about to place his feet on the wide porch when a buckboard rattled up the street. He glanced automatically and was slightly surprised to see Jane Blain.

The girl was driving the pair. She was dressed in her range garb of brown shirt and blue levis, boots and wide-brimmed Stetson. She immediately halted the buckboard beside the sheriff and jumped down and almost ran to him.

"Oh, Sheriff! I'd like to talk to you!"

"Yeah, Miss Jane?"

She paused, spoke more evenly, quietly.

"Have you seen my brother? Has he entered town today?"

Tom Hudson hesitated; then said harshly:

"Nope. I ain't seen him. Why?"

"I feel restless," said the girl

worriedly. "I don't like Rory being away from the ranch. I wish I could talk to him. He rode away with — with — some other men. I've wondered if he entered town."

"Take a look around," said Tom Hudson heavily. "I got work to do."

"Have you seen Chet Wayne? I saw him ridin' out but I've wondered if he got back to town."

"I ain't seen that hombre."

Even as he snapped the sour words, he realized the girl could be suspicious if she made further inquiries.

Because Chet Wayne and Ezra Sloan had been seen by many riding into town with the three Mexican prisoners. It was possible someone had seen Chet and Ezra walk into the Bonanza Hotel with Sheriff Tom Hudson, too.

Angry and disgruntled he turned and walked away from the girl.

Jane stared at his retreating back.

"Well, what's wrong with him!" she exclaimed.

She walked back to the buckboard,

stood deep in thought for a moment. A wisp of hair coiled down. She pushed it back under her hat absent-mindedly. Her brown, clear face was serious. She wished earnestly she had someone to help her. That someone, she thought, could well be big, handsome Chet Wayne! But first she had to find him, and if Tom Hudson would not help she intended to make inquiries herself.

She had an inward restlessness. She wanted to do something about Rory. She had seen Chet Wayne and Ezra Sloan ride off after her brother and his wild companions. She just had an intense desire to know what was happening. It was possible, she thought, that Chet had returned to Laredo.

She climbed to the buckboard and gripped the ribbons. She set the pair jogging down the street.

Some fifteen minutes later Jane had possession of some strange information.

In the first place, she met up with two elderly women, wives of store-keepers. They told her how the deputy had been observed riding in with three Mexicans who were obviously prisoners, and that they had been taken to the jail.

"Yes, my gal, that young feller shore knows how to handle these danged badmen."

"Jest what this town needs, if yuh ask me," said the other woman. "Time we had a strong sheriff, if yuh git what I mean, my dearie. And ain't Chet Wayne a-been a-visiting you?"

"Yes — er, yes!" stammered Jane. "But not lately. Thanks for everything you've told me!"

She got away, leaving the gossips with something to weave conjectures around!

Jane drove the buckboard straight back to the sheriff's office. Without any further ado, she walked down the passage, knocked an the office door and promptly walked in.

Tom Hudson was standing before the barred cells, the bunch of keys in his hand. Startled, he swung around when he realized the door had opened.

"What d'yuh want?"

"I'd like to talk to you, Tom Hudson!"

He lumbered away from the cells and hung the keys up on the nail.

"I thought we had a talk not so long ago."

"Shore." She spoke bitingly. "Yuh told me you'd not seen Chet Wayne. Well, I know that's untrue. Chet Wayne rode into town with those three Mexicans. Why are yuh tellin' me lies, Tom Hudson?"

He leaned back against his desk.

"Who yuh been talkin' to?"

"Some of the folks in town. They saw Chet Wayne and his pardner ride in. You must have known that, too, else how d'yuh account for these three hombres? Why tell me lies?"

"I'm tryin' to protect yuh!" said the other harshly.

"Where is Chet Wayne? What do yuh mean — yuh're tryin' to protect me?"

He was suddenly lost for words. He

knew nothing he could say would allay her suspicions. He lumbered away from her and stared out of a window.

One of the Mexicans suddenly sang out.

"Señor Sheriff, you were going to set us free! Why don't you get on with it?"

Tom Hudson turned with an unintelligible snarl. Then, realizing the futility of bluff, he swung back to staring savagely out of the window.

Jane's quick mind seized on the words.

"Why should yuh set them free? Why did Chet bring them in, anyway?"

"Miss Jane, there's things yuh don't know much about!" said Tom Hudson thickly.

"You can tell me," she urged.

"Yuh got a wild hellion brother!" he rasped. "An' he's in the pay of Luke Starn."

"I know that," she said quietly.

"Yuh don't know that Luke Starn has me hog-tied the same way!" he snapped,

334

his armour of secrecy breaking down at last.

"I can guess."

Tom Hudson gripped the butts of his guns.

"What's Chet Wayne to yuh, Miss Jane? Do yuh want to be his wife?"

"If he asks me — yes!"

"Yuh love thet galoot?"

"Yes, I love him."

Tom Hudson reached for his hat and gripped it until it was almost shapeless.

"I guess this is the end o' the trail for me!" he muttered. "But I aim to fix things right afore I ride out of this town." He paused, said in a stronger voice: "Come with me. We're goin' to rescue Chet Wayne an' that old coot who trails around with him. We're gittin' him out o' thet Bonanza Hotel, and after that I reckon there ain't much more I got to do."

"Where is he? What danger is he in?"

"Wal, right now he's lyin' hog-tied in a room at the Bonanza Hotel. Him an' thet old coot. Luke Starn an' yore hot-head brother fixed him thataway. Those two rannigans are aimin' to bring a herd o' stolen beef down to yore ranch, and they want Chet Wayne and thet old gink out o' the way while they do it." Tom Hudson gave a grating laugh. "Shore seems like Chet bust up those rannigans up in the hills an' then brought these three pesky rustlers down hyar as prisoners. I ain't got nothin' against Chet Wayne an' right now I know I can't trust Luke Starn. I'm a blamed fool! He'll kill Chet as soon as he figgers it's convenient!"

"We've got to go over to that hotel!" cried Jane.

Tom Hudson nodded, patted his guns and strode to the door. Now that he had decided on his fate, he seemed a different man.

"Let's git! But watch yore step, Miss Jane."

They walked the distance to the Bonanza Hotel. They wended through dusty streets, past men and women who moved idly in the heat little realizing the grim emotions of Sheriff Tom Hudson and the girl.

They approached the drab Bonanza Hotel, but did not hesitate. Tom Hudson walked in ahead of the girl. His hands hovered on gun butts.

But once again the hotel seemed very quiet. Perhaps Luke Starn had arranged it so that the place was to be deserted that afternoon. There was no sign of the manager. Tom Hudson moved resolutely to the staircase, and Jane followed.

Sheriff Tom Hudson knew what he was doing. He was bringing to a climax Luke Starn's attempt at domination in Laredo. He was also bringing his own career to a disgraceful close. In fact, if he got away from Laredo with a whole skin, he would be lucky.

But now there was only one impulse in his grim mind. He was setting Chet Wayne free, and the young deputy would have the task of settling with Luke Starn and his hirelings.

He did not think there would be

anyone in the room on the landing except the two bound men. Right now he figured Luke Starn and Rory Blain were out fixing up for more men to replace those lost in the hills. They would need a good trail crew if they wanted to get those steers down out of the badlands.

As he expected, the door of the room was locked. He motioned Jane to one side. He hunched his shoulders and pressed his iron-hard weight against the door.

The door was not very strong; the lock tore splinters out of the surrounding woodwork. Then the whole thing flew in. Tom Hudson steadied and walked into the room, guns in hands.

The setup was just as he had expected. Chet Wayne and oldster Ezra Sloan were lying on the floor, bound with manila and with dirty handkerchiefs stuffed in their mouths and tied so that they were immovable.

But the men's eyes lit up in surprise as the sheriff and the girl walked in.

Jane dropped on her knees beside Chet Wayne. At once her hands were busy with the gag. There was only one trouble — she could not tackle Ezra's gag at the same time! She hoped he would understand!

There was one thing the girl missed. And that was the fact that Tom Hudson quietly withdrew from the room the moment he figured that Chet and Ezra were near to freedom and responsibility for their own safety.

He went quietly down the stairs. He walked swiftly around the block and made for the livery.

He intended to get his horse, money and rifle, grub and saddle-bag and light out of Laredo for ever!

Back in the bare hotel room, Jane worked furiously on Chet Wayne's gag. The first very spasm of anger had actually hindered her. She had made no progress. But now she rapidly loosened the cloths and threw them away. She went to work on the ropes.

Chet had regained consciousness some

time ago. And with the loosening of the gag, he became voluble.

"Say, how come Tom Hudson bust in here like that, Jane?"

"Oh, he's changed! He told me a lot about Luke Starn."

"Wal, the buzzard led us to this trap!" said Chet grimly. "Never mind. I jest want my hands free an' my guns back in the leather."

The Colts had been taken out of his holsters and stacked on a shelf high up on one wall. The same thing had happened to Ezra Sloan's gun.

Jane got the rope off Chet's hands. She wished she had a knife. Chet waved her to one side while he tackled Ezra's gag and bonds. His hard fingers soon made quick work of the restraints.

Ezra was pretty near choking when the gags were finally got out of his mouth — but it was mostly because he was prevented from using his wide range of cuss words because of the girl's presence!

Then Chet went to work with expert

fingers on Ezra's bound hands. Soon the old-timer was able to tackle his own knots which still bound his feet. Chet worked on his own bindings which were around his ankles. In some minutes, while Jane kneeled beside them, they were completely free.

"There's a lot I don't understand," gritted Chet Wayne. "How come Tom Hudson brought yuh here? He tricked us. He was the hombre who got us up here an' he knew he was leadin' us to a trap."

"There are plenty of things I don't understand, too," cried Jane. "I don't know what happened after you rode away from the Double X. But I'm glad you're safe. Luke Starn would have returned here to murder you, I'm shore!"

"Durned tootin' he would!" roared Ezra. "It's a wonder that snakeroo didn't kill us right away!"

Chet lurched over to the shelf and got his guns. He shoved his guns into the holsters; made sure they were slack.

He handed Ezra his old Colt.

"Those hombres are in town, shore thing!" he said curtly.

They had hardly holstered the guns when a step sounded outside in the passage.

Someone pushed on the door — and when it opened to the touch, there was an exclamation of surprise.

Framed in the doorway was Rory Blain. His startled face surveyed the scene inside the room for less than a split second.

Then his hands scooped for his guns.

Chet Wayne hesitated for the first time in any gun emergency.

He had every reason for that awful hesitation which, however, lasted for an unmeasurable moment of time. The man before him was Jane's brother! Fate had thrown him into a gun-battle against the girl's brother before her very eyes!

Guns exploded and concussion filled the air. The smell of gunsmoke drifted lazily.

If Chet Wayne had reason to hesitate terribly, Ezra Sloan had not.

The old-timer had scooped as fast for his solitary hogleg as Rory Blain had gone for his guns.

Words and explanations had been dropped utterly before raw, violent action. There was no need for anything but swift deadly gun-play.

A slug caught Ezra Sloan in the right shoulder and he dropped his gun. But his Colt had roared. The gun had done its fatal work.

Rory Blain rammed back under the impact of the slug from Ezra's Colt. That movement had deflected his guns. One slug had gone wide, and the other had hit Ezra in the shoulder.

But Rory Blain was already dead, even as he slid down the wall, his expression changing from living hatred to a rigid mask.

Chet Wayne had not fired his guns at all.

Rory Blain had a hole in his forehead from which a reddish mess oozed.

Jane screamed. Chet slid guns to holsters and held her. She covered her face. She did not want to look at the thing that had once been her brother.

"Let's git out o' here!" grated Chet Wayne. He stared at Ezra. "Yuh all right? Kin yuh walk?"

"I reckon so," mumbled the oldster. Pain was jagging through him, but his shoulder was already numb. "Ain't no more than a pesky scratch. Reckon I fixed thet jigger. He was set to git yuh. An' he would ha' done. Yuh ain't fired them irons."

"Thanks to yuh, I didn't have to," said Chet slowly. "All right. Yuh need a Doc. An' I want Jane out o' here. Do we stand yappin' all day, old-timer?"

They walked out of the room. Chet had to almost force Jane away. There was nothing she could do for her wild brother. He had died by the gun — as he had lived!

They got out of the hotel and moved along the dusty road. Ezra Sloan lurched a bit. A crowd straggled along behind them. The folks sensed something was afoot.

Fortunately, Doc Harper appeared quickly. As it happened, his house was not far from the scene. He walked back to the sheriff's office with Chet. When they got there the Doc forced old Ezra Sloan to receive some medical attention. A few words and the Doc knew that Rory Blain was dead.

On the desk, in the sheriff's office, was a very brief note. It ran:

'Chet: I'm taking the trail. Luke Starn had me over the Bar 2 Bar horses. Get that hombre. I ain't got the guts.'

The note was unsigned.

Chet Wayne crumpled it into a ball and pushed it into his shirt pocket. No one else seen had the note. He thought if Tom Hudson was riding out, alone and conscience-stricken at his age, that was probably enough punishment.

The work that followed during the

next hour was mostly work for a doctor. Rory Blain was taken from the death-room. Ezra was patched up and pronounced hard as old railroad iron.

There was more pleasant work for Chet Wayne in explaining to Jane that he had not shot Rory Blain.

"I'm glad I didn't trigger!"

"I wouldn't have blamed yuh if yuh had," she said quietly. "And I don't blame Ezra. He decided to save your life. That means a — a lot to me, Chet!"

That night, after fruitless inquiries concerning Luke Starn, Chet heard from a caller that the desperado was back in town.

Chet Wayne had concluded that Rory Blain had returned to the Bonanza Hotel for no other reason than to kill the man he hated. Luke Starn had apparently not ordered the visit.

Luke Starn had been out of town — probably on arrangements connected with the trail crew. But now he was back in town. He would know that

Rory Blain was dead. In which case, the man's return was sheer bravado.

After the caller had gone, Chet Wayne rose from the desk where he had been writing a report. He was not yet the sheriff but if the office was offered him, he would accept. He thought it probable that he would be elected.

As Ezra Sloan was resting — compulsorily — and Jane was back at the Double X, with a kindly wife to afford comfort and company, Chet Wayne had no one to answer to.

He reached for his Stetson. He doused the lamp and walked out of the building, locking the doors behind him.

As he walked along in the semi-darkness he hitched his gun-belt in a more comfortable position.

He knew he was going out to kill Luke Starn or arrest him. If the man agreed to arrest, a case would be built up against him. But — Chet figured Luke Starn would go for a gun!

He found the man in the Gold Nugget, blandly buying drinks and fondling a pack of playing cards. The man was dressed in a city-made suit of black. It was a typical gambler's suit, traditional to the type. But the first thing that Chet noticed was that Luke Starn was wearing no guns.

Chet thought grimly there was to be no gun-play.

A hush fell over the saloon as Chet walked in and stood some yards away from Luke Starn. Chet's immobile face under his wide-brimmed hat caught a shaft of light and looked stern.

"I aim to arrest yuh, Luke Starn. As Deputy Sheriff, in the absence of Sheriff Hudson, I have power to arrest yuh on charge of murder, robbery and rustling."

Men moved stealthily away from the bar counter. But Luke Starn had his own brand of iron-hard guts.

"That's a powerful lot o' charges, Deputy."

"Are yuh comin' or . . . " Chet did not finish the question. Instead his eyes flickered to the other's gunless waist.

"I got no alternative seemingly!" said the other harshly.

Suspicion flamed through Chet Wayne, but he could not see how Luke Starn could get the drop on him.

"All right. Let's walk!" snapped the deputy.

Luke Starn drank his whisky coolly and then started forward.

"Anythin' yuh say," he murmured. "I figger yuh're making a mistake, that's all."

Chet Wayne moved up behind him as they passed through the bat-wing doors and out into the semi-dark of the street.

They had hardly got past the hitching-rail when Luke Starn made his play — and a cunning play it was!

Apparently he had not believed that Chet Wayne would make a charge against him. Maybe his ego had given him that belief. But now that there was no alternative but imprisonment or fight, he chose to fight — and he had one of the west's most cunning weapons.

He wheeled swiftly, drawing at the same time.

Chet scooped faster than the speed of light. He knew in a flash that Luke Starn was using a hidden derringer.

The spring-loaded little gun, hidden in a strap up the man's sleeve in the typical manner of the crook gambler, flashed in the night. But Chet Wayne's Colts were drawn with the speed of magic. Practice beat cunning.

The bark of the derringer was drowned in the roar of Colts. Flame spat in the night, and it came from Chet's guns. Slugs tore out and found a target. The one bullet that fired from the derringer tore through thin air inches above Chet's shoulder.

The young deputy watched the man sprawl back under the terrible impact of two Colt slugs. Death, almost instant, was there.

Chet Wayne just walked away, legs steady and head cool. The task was finished. Others could take the corpse to boothill.

Chet wanted to think and relax. More, he wanted to see Jane and get around to talking of decent, peaceful things.

There were constructive things to do. He would not hang up his guns because bringing law and order to Laredo was constructive; but he thought that marrying the right sort of gal was one good thing a man could do!

That was what he wanted to think about; marrying Jane and doing other things besides hunt those who chose the owl-hoot trail.

Other titles in the
Linford Western Library:

TOP HAND
Wade Everett

The Broken T was big. But no ranch is big enough to let a man hide from himself.

GUN WOLVES OF LOBO BASIN
Lee Floren

The Feud was a blood debt. When Smoke Talbot found the outlaws who gunned down his folks he aimed to nail their hide to the barn door.

SHOTGUN SHARKEY
Marshall Grover

The westbound coach carrying the indomitable Larry and Stretch headed for a shooting showdown.

ARIZONA DRIFTERS
W. C. Tuttle

When drifting Dutton and Lonnie Steelman decide to become partners they find that they have a common enemy in the formidable Thurston brothers.

TOMBSTONE
Matt Braun

Wells Fargo paid Luke Starbuck to outgun the silver-thieving stagecoach gang at Tombstone. Before long Luke can see the only thing bearing fruit in this eldorado will be the gallows tree.

HIGH BORDER RIDERS
Lee Floren

Buckshot McKee and Tortilla Joe cut the trail of a border tough who was running Mexican beef into Texas. They stopped the smuggler in his tracks.

BRETT RANDALL, GAMBLER
E. B. Mann

Larry Day had the choice of running away from the law or of assuming a dead man's place. No matter what he decided he was bound to end up dead.

THE GUNSHARP
William R. Cox

The Eggerleys weren't very smart. They trained their sights on Will Carney and Arizona's biggest blood bath began.

THE DEPUTY OF SAN RIANO
Lawrence A. Keating and
Al. P. Nelson

When a man fell dead from his horse, Ed Grant was spotted riding away from the scene. The deputy sheriff rode out after him and came up against everything from gunfire to dynamite.

FARGO: MASSACRE RIVER
John Benteen

The ambushers up ahead had now blocked the road. Fargo's convoy was a jumble, a perfect target for the insurgents' weapons!

SUNDANCE: DEATH IN THE LAVA
John Benteen

The Modoc's captured the wagon train and its cargo of gold. But now the halfbreed they called Sundance was going after it . . .

HARSH RECKONING
Phil Ketchum

Five years of keeping himself alive in a brutal prison had made Brand tough and careless about who he gunned down . . .

FARGO: PANAMA GOLD
John Benteen

With foreign money behind him, Buckner was going to destroy the Panama Canal before it could be completed. Fargo's job was to stop Buckner.

FARGO: THE SHARPSHOOTERS
John Benteen

The Canfield clan, thirty strong were raising hell in Texas. Fargo was tough enough to hold his own against the whole clan.

PISTOL LAW
Paul Evan Lehman

Lance Jones came back to Mustang for just one thing — revenge! Revenge on the people who had him thrown in jail.

HELL RIDERS
Steve Mensing

Wade Walker's kid brother, Duane, was locked up in the Silver City jail facing a rope at dawn. Wade was a ruthless outlaw, but he was smart, and he had vowed to have his brother out of jail before morning!

DESERT OF THE DAMNED
Nelson Nye

The law was after him for the murder of a marshal — a murder he didn't commit. Breen was after him for revenge — and Breen wouldn't stop at anything . . . blackmail, a frameup . . . or murder.

DAY OF THE COMANCHEROS
Steven C. Lawrence

Their very name struck terror into men's hearts — the Comancheros, a savage army of cutthroats who swept across Texas, leaving behind a blood-stained trail of robbery and murder.

SUNDANCE: SILENT ENEMY
John Benteen

A lone crazed Cheyenne was on a personal war path. They needed to pit one man against one crazed Indian. That man was Sundance.

LASSITER
Jack Slade

Lassiter wasn't the kind of man to listen to reason. Cross him once and he'll hold a grudge for years to come — if he let you live that long.

LAST STAGE TO GOMORRAH
Barry Cord

Jeff Carter, tough ex-riverboat gambler, now had himself a horse ranch that kept him free from gunfights and card games. Until Sturvesant of Wells Fargo showed up.

McALLISTER ON THE COMANCHE CROSSING
Matt Chisholm

The Comanche, McAllister owes them a life — and the trail is soaked with the blood of the men who had tried to outrun them before.

QUICK-TRIGGER COUNTRY
Clem Colt

Turkey Red hooked up with Curly Bill Graham's outlaw crew. But wholesale murder was out of Turk's line, so when range war flared he bucked the whole border gang alone . . .

CAMPAIGNING
Jim Miller

Ambushed on the Santa Fe trail, Sean Callahan is saved by two Indian strangers. But there'll be more lead and arrows flying before the band join Kit Carson against the Comanches.

GUNSLINGER'S RANGE
Jackson Cole

Three escaped convicts are out for revenge. They won't rest until they put a bullet through the head of the dirty snake who locked them behind bars.

RUSTLER'S TRAIL
Lee Floren

Jim Carlin knew he would have to stand up and fight because he had staked his claim right in the middle of Big Ike Outland's best grass.

THE TRUTH ABOUT SNAKE RIDGE
Marshall Grover

The troubleshooters came to San Cristobal to help the needy. For Larry and Stretch the turmoil began with a brawl and then an ambush.

WOLF DOG RANGE
Lee Floren

Will Ardery would stop at nothing, unless something stopped him first — like a bullet from Pete Manly's gun.

DEVIL'S DINERO
Marshall Grover

Plagued by remorse, a rich old reprobate hired the Texas Troubleshooters to deliver a fortune in greenbacks to each of his victims.

GUNS OF FURY
Ernest Haycox

Dane Starr, alias Dan Smith, wanted to close the door on his past and hang up his guns, but people wouldn't let him.

DONOVAN
Elmer Kelton

Donovan was supposed to be dead. Uncle Joe Vickers had fired off both barrels of a shotgun into the vicious outlaw's face as he was escaping from jail. Now Uncle Joe had been shot — in just the same way.

CODE OF THE GUN
Gordon D. Shirreffs

MacLean came riding home, with saddle tramp written all over him, but sewn in his shirt-lining was an Arizona Ranger's star.

GAMBLER'S GUN LUCK
Brett Austen

Gamblers seldom live long. Parker was a hell of a gambler. It was his life — or his death ...